PENGUIN BOOKS
1841
AIMEZ-VOUS BRAHMS...
FRANÇOISE SAGAN

AIMEZ-VOUS BRAHMS...

Françoise Sagan

TRANSLATED BY
PETER WILES

*

PENGUIN BOOKS

Penguin Books Ltd, Harmondsworth, Middlesex
AUSTRALIA: Penguin Books Pty Ltd, 762 Whitehorse Road,
Mitcham, Victoria

—

First published 1959
Published in Great Britain by John Murray 1960
Published in Penguin Books 1962

—

Copyright © Françoise Sagan, 1959
English translation copyright © John Murray 1960

—

Made and printed in Great Britain
by Hazell Watson & Viney Ltd,
Aylesbury and Slough
Set in Monotype Garamond

TO GUY

I

PAULE gazed at her face in the mirror and studied the accumulated defeats of thirty-nine years, one by one, not with the panic, the acrimony usual at such times, but with a detached calm. As though the tepid skin, which her two fingers plucked now and then to accentuate a wrinkle or bring out a shadow, belonged to someone else, to another Paule passionately concerned with her beauty and battling with the transition from young to youngish woman: a woman she scarcely recognized. She had stationed herself at this mirror to kill time only to discover – she smiled at the thought – that time was gradually, painlessly killing her, aiming its blows at an appearance she knew had been loved.

Roger was due at nine; it was now seven; she had plenty of time. Time to lie back on her bed with her eyes shut, to think of nothing. To give way. To relax. But what was so engrossing, so taxing about her days as to warrant rest in the evenings? And well she knew this uneasy listlessness which drove her from room to room, window to window. It belonged to the wet days of her childhood.

She went into the bathroom and bent down to feel the water in the bath, and suddenly the gesture reminded her of another ... Nearly fifteen years before. She was with Marc, they were spending their holidays together for the second year running and already she felt it couldn't last. They were on Marc's sailing-boat; the sail fluttered in the wind like an uncertain heart; she was twenty-five. And suddenly she had felt overcome by happiness, accepting everything in her life, accepting the world, realizing in a flash that everything was fine. And to hide her face she had bent over the gunwale, trying to dip her fingers in the racing water. The little craft had heeled over; Marc had given her one of those dead-pan looks he was so good at and, inside her, happiness had at once been replaced by a sense of irony. Of course, she had been happy afterwards, with or by means of others, but never in the same total, irreplaceable manner. And in the final analysis it was like looking back on a broken promise.

*

Roger was coming; she would explain to him; she would try to explain to him. He would say: 'Yes, of course,' with the particular satisfaction he invariably showed in laying bare life's impostures, a real enthusiasm for expatiating on the absurdity of existence, of their stubbornness in prolonging it. Only, in him all this was compensated by boundless vitality, keen appetites, and, at bottom, a vast natural contentment which only sleep interrupted. Then he would drop off at a moment's notice, hand over heart, as attentive to his life in sleeping as in waking. No, she could not explain to Roger that she was tired, that she could stand no more of this freedom imposed like a law between them, this freedom of which he alone availed himself and which for her represented mere loneliness; she could not tell him that sometimes she felt like one of those ruthless, possessive females whom he so hated. Abruptly her deserted flat struck her as odious and useless.

At nine o'clock Roger rang and, opening the door, finding him there, smiling and rather massive, she told herself resignedly, all over again, that here was her fate and she loved it. He took her in his arms.

'What a wonderful dress you're wearing . . . I've missed you. Are you alone?'

'Yes. Come in.'

Are you alone . . .? Suppose she had answered: 'No, you've picked the wrong time'? But in six years she never had. He still asked and occasionally apologized for disturbing her, exhibiting a guile which pained her more than his inconstancy. (He could not even admit the possibility of her being lonely and unhappy because of him.) She smiled at him. He opened a bottle, poured two drinks, sat down.

'Come over here next to me, Paule. Where would you like us to eat?'

She sat next to him. He too looked tired. He took her hand and squeezed it.

'I'm up to my neck in problems,' he said. 'The business world is crazy, people are too stupid and spineless for words. Oh, for a quiet country life . . .'

She laughed.

'You'd be lost without your Quai-de-Bercy and your warehouses and your lorries. And your long nights in Paris . . .'

9

At this final phrase he smiled, stretched, and flopped out on the divan. She did not turn. She looked at the hand he had left in hers; a broad, open hand. She was familiar with every bit of him, his thick, sleeked-down hair, the exact expression of his somewhat prominent blue eyes, the curve of his mouth. She knew him by heart.

'While we're on the subject,' he said, 'while we're on the subject of my midnight orgies, I was run in like a hoodlum the other evening. I'd got into a brawl. Me . . . in my forties . . . taken round to the station. I ask you!'

'What were you fighting about?'

'I can't remember. But the other fellow got the worst of it.'

And as though the memory of this show of strength had given him new life, he leapt from the divan.

'I know where we'll go,' he said. 'The Piémontais. Afterwards we'll go dancing. If you're ready to allow I can dance.'

'You don't dance,' said Paule, 'you shuffle.'

'That isn't everyone's opinion.'

'If you're referring to the poor young things you enslave,' said Paule, 'that is another matter.'

They laughed. Roger's little adventures were a great joke between them. Paule leaned against the wall for a moment before reaching for the banister. She felt thoroughly dejected.

In Roger's car, she absent-mindedly switched on the radio. For a second she caught a glimpse of her hand, long and beautifully kept, by the wan light of the dashboard. The veins stood out on the back, campaigning up towards the fingers, mingling in an irregular pattern. Like a picture of my life, she thought, then at once reflected that the picture was a false one. She had a job she liked, a past she could look back on without regrets, good friends. And a lasting alliance. She turned to Roger.

'How many times have I done this before – turned on your car radio as you've driven me off to dinner?'

'I couldn't say.'

He shot her a sidelong glance. Despite the passage of time and his certainty of her love for him, he remained astonishingly sensitive to her moods, always on the alert. Just as in the early days. She checked a 'Do you remember?' and decided to keep close watch on her sentimentality for the rest of the evening.

'Does the action feel stale?'

'No. It's I who feel a bit stale at times.'

He reached towards her; she clasped his hand in hers. He was driving fast, the familiar streets raced beneath the car, Paris shone with autumn rain. He laughed.

'I wonder what makes me drive so fast? I'm afraid it's a case of acting young.'

She did not answer. He had been acting young for as long as she had known him. It was only lately he had confessed as much, and this very confession scared her. She was becoming increasingly scared of the role of confidante into which – from fondness, understanding – she was slipping. He was her life, he was forgetting the fact and she was helping him to forget it, with commendable self-effacement.

They dined quietly, discussing the worries which were bound to arise in a road transport concern like Roger's, then she told him two or three amusing anecdotes about the shops she was decorating. One of Fath's customers was crying out for her to make something of her flat. An American, fairly rich.

'Van den Besh?' said Roger. 'That rings a bell. Oh yes . . .'

She raised her eyebrows. He wore the sprightly look which memories of a certain category always aroused in him.

'I used to know her in the old days. Before the war, I'm afraid. She was always dining in Florence's.'

'Since when, she's been married and divorced and all the rest of it.'

'Ah yes,' he said dreamily, 'her name was, er . . .'

He was beginning to get on her nerves. She had a sudden desire to dig her fork into the palm of his hand.

'Her Christian name is of no concern to me,' she said. 'I believe she has a fair bit of money and no taste. Exactly what I need to keep the wolf from the door.'

'How old is she?'

'In her sixties,' she said coldly, and seeing Roger's expression she burst out laughing. He leaned across the table and looked her in the eyes.

'You're perfectly horrible. You go out of your

way to depress me. I love you just the same, but I shouldn't.'

He liked making out he was hard done by. She sighed.

'Anyway, I'm calling on her tomorrow. Avenue Kléber. I'm getting alarmingly short of money. And so are you,' she added briskly as his hand moved upwards.

'Let's talk about something else,' he said. 'Let's go and dance for a while.'

In the night club, they sat at a small table far from the floor and watched the procession of faces without a word. She held his hand in hers, she felt perfectly secure, perfectly attuned to him. The effort of getting to know someone new would be altogether beyond her, and she derived a doleful happiness from this conviction. They danced. He held her firmly, advancing the length of the floor without rhythm, looking very pleased with himself. She was very happy.

Later they drove back, he got out of the car and took her in his arms in the porchway.

'I'll let you sleep. See you tomorrow, darling.'

He kissed her lightly and drove off. She waved her hand. He was letting her sleep more and more often. Her flat was empty and she meticulously arranged her things before sitting down on the bed with tears in her eyes. She was alone again tonight, and her life to come appeared to her as a long succession of lonely nights, in sheets which would never be rumpled, in the unimpeachable dullness of a long convalescence. In bed, she reached out instinctively as though there were a warm flank to touch, she breathed softly as though for fear of waking somebody – man or child. Anyone who needed her, needed her warmth awake and asleep. But nobody really needed her. Roger, perhaps, on and off ... But not really. Not in the purely physiological, passion-free way in which she had sometimes known need. She brooded gently, bitterly, on her loneliness.

*

Roger parked his car outside his door and walked for some time. He took deep breaths and gradually lengthened his stride. He felt good. He felt good whenever he saw Paule, he loved no one but her. Only, tonight as he was leaving her he had sensed her sadness and had not known what to say. That she was confusedly asking him for something, something which he could not give her, which he had never been able to give anyone, he knew well enough. No doubt he should have stayed and made love to her; that was still the best way of reassuring a woman. But he had a hankering to stretch his legs, roam the streets, go prowling. He had a hankering to hear the sound of his footsteps on the pavement, to watch over this town he knew so well, maybe to catch its late-night windfalls. He made for the lights down by the river.

2

SHE woke dog-tired and late, and left in a rush. She had to call on that American on her way to the office. At ten o'clock she entered a half-empty drawing-room in the Avenue Kléber and, since the lady of the house was still asleep, quietly went over her make-up in front of the mirror. It was in the mirror she saw Simon coming. He was wearing an outsize dressing-gown; he was tousled and strikingly handsome. Not my type, she thought, still without turning, and she smiled at herself for a moment. He was very slim, very dark, with limpid eyes – rather lanky.

He did not see her at first and made for the window, humming to himself. She coughed and he turned guiltily towards her. For a moment she thought this must be Mrs Van den Besh's latest fancy.

'I beg your pardon,' he said, 'I didn't see you. I'm Simon Van den Besh.'

'Your mother asked me to call in this morning and take a look at her flat. I'm afraid I've roused the whole household.'

'Ah well, one has to get up sooner or later,' he said sadly. And she thought with weariness: he's the whimpering kind.

'Do sit down,' he said, solemnly seating himself opposite her and pulling his dressing-gown closer about him.

He looked rather cowed. Paule began to experience a faint liking for him. At all events, he did not seem unduly conscious of his looks: this was unhoped for.

'I suppose it's still raining?'

She laughed. She was thinking of the look on Roger's face if he could see her sitting here with professional poise, terrorizing an over-endowed young creature, in his dressing-gown, at ten in the morning.

'Oh yes, it's still raining,' she said gaily.

He glanced up.

'What do you expect me to say?' he said. 'I don't know you. If I did, I'd tell you how happy I was to see you again.'

She stared at him, taken aback.

'Why?'

'I just would.'

He looked away. She found him odder and odder.

'This flat could certainly do with a bit more furniture,' she said. 'Where do you sit when there are more than three of you?'

'I don't know,' he said. 'I'm seldom here. I'm out at work all day and I come home so tired that I go straight to bed.'

Paule was losing all her preconceptions. He did not parade his looks; he worked all day. She nearly asked: 'What do you do?' but she restrained herself. Such inquisitiveness was unlike her.

'I'm devilling for a barrister,' pursued Simon. 'It's a hard life: working till midnight, up at dawn . . .'

'It's ten o'clock,' Paule pointed out.

'My chief client went to the guillotine this morning,' he said languidly.

She gave a start. He kept his eyes lowered.

'Good heavens!' she said. 'You mean ... he's dead?'

The pair of them burst out laughing. He rose and took a cigarette from the mantel-shelf.

'No, actually I don't do much work – not enough. Whereas you ... Up at ten, all set to furnish this frightful room. I'm overawed.'

He strode up and down, looking very worked up.

'Take it easy,' said Paule.

She felt in excellent spirits, thoroughly restored. She also began to dread the arrival of Simon's mother.

'I'll go and put some clothes on,' said Simon. 'It won't take a minute. Do wait for me.'

*

She spent an hour making lavish plans with Mrs Van den Besh, visibly disgruntled and rather haggard in the morning, and came downstairs in raptures, mapping out her finances and completely forgetful of Simon's existence. Outside, it was still raining. She raised her hand to call a taxi, and a small, low-slung car stopped in front of her. Simon opened the door.

'Can I drop you off? I was just leaving for the office.'

He had obviously been waiting for an hour, but his artful look melted Paule. She bent double, struggled in, and smiled.

'I'm going to the Avenue Matignon.'

'Did you settle things with my mother?'

'Admirably. You'll soon have downy couches to rest your weary limbs. You're sure I shan't be making you too late? It's gone eleven. They've had time to send everyone to the guillotine.'

'I've plenty of time,' he said sullenly.

'I'm not getting at you,' she resumed gently. 'I feel in good form because until today I had money troubles, and thanks to your mother I can say good-bye to them.'

'Make her pay up before you start,' he said. 'She's as mean as they come.'

'That's no way to speak of one's parents,' said Paule.

'I'm not a kid of twelve.'

'How old *are* you?'

'Twenty-five. And you?'

'Thirty-nine.'

He gave a low whistle, so rude that for a split second she was close to losing her temper; then she roared with laughter.

'What are you laughing at?'

'The admiring whistle . . .'

'It was much more admiring than you think,' he said, and he looked at her so tenderly that she felt embarrassed.

The windscreen-wipers beat time with supreme inefficacy and she wondered how he was able to drive. She had laddered one of her stockings getting in; she felt marvellously gay in this uncomfortable car, with this young and clearly captivated stranger and the rain trickling down from the hood and soiling her light-coloured coat. She began to hum: after paying her taxes, after posting off her mother's allowance and settling her debts at the shop, she would have . . . she didn't feel like working it out. Simon was another fast driver. She thought of Roger and the night she had spent and grew gloomy again.

'You wouldn't care to have lunch with me one day?'

Simon spoke quickly, without looking at her. She felt a momentary panic. She did not know him; it would mean making efforts at conversation, asking him questions about himself, entering a new existence. She rebelled at the idea.

'I can't at the moment. I've too much work.'

'Ah,' he said.

He did not insist. She shot a glance at him, he had slowed down and seemed even to be driving sadly. She took a cigarette and he held out his lighter. He had boyish wrists; they were too thin and projected comically from a heavy tweed jacket. You shouldn't dress like a trapper with your build, she thought, and she had a momentary hankering to take him in hand. He was just the type to arouse maternal instincts in a woman of her age.

'Here we are,' she said.

He got out without a word and opened the door for her. He looked mulish and downcast.

'Thank you again,' she said.

'It was nothing.'

She took three paces towards the door and turned. He had not moved. He was looking at her.

3

SIMON spent a quarter of an hour looking for a space and finally parked six hundred yards from his office. He was devilling for a friend of his mother's, a very famous and entirely odious barrister who, for reasons Simon dreaded understanding, put up with his nonsense. There were times when he felt like pushing him too far, but his laziness deterred him. Stepping out on to the pavement he stumbled and at once began to limp, looking meek and resigned. Women turned as he passed and Simon felt their thoughts hit him in the back: 'So young, so handsome – and a cripple! How tragic!', though he derived no assurance from his looks, only relief: 'I'd never have had the strength to be ugly.' And the thought brought in its wake a glimpse of an ascetic life: now the outcast painter, now the shepherd in the blazing Landes.

He limped into the office, and old Alice shot him a glance which was part solicitous, part sceptical. She knew his pet diversions and suffered them with regretful condescension. Had he taken his work seriously he might, with his looks and his imagination, have become a great advocate. He made her a grandiloquent bow and sat down at his desk.

'Why the limp?'

'It isn't a proper limp. Who killed who last

night? When am I going to have a nice, fat, juicy murder to deal with?'

'You've been buzzed for three times this morning. It's half past eleven.'

The buzzer could only be the Grand Maître. Simon glanced at the door.

'I overslept. But I met someone really terrific.'

'A woman?'

'Yes. You know: lovely face, very soft, a little drawn ... gestures which were really gestures ... Afflicted with some secret sorrow ...'

'Your time would be better spent looking at the Guillaut file.'

'Of course.'

'Is she married?'

Simon was jerked out of his dreams.

'I don't know ... But if she is, they're not happy. She's been having money troubles, but they cleared up this morning and she was so gay. I love women who delight in money.'

She shrugged.

'Then you love them all.'

'Nearly all,' said Simon. 'Except when they're too young.'

He immersed himself in his file. The door opened and Maître Fleury's head appeared.

'Monsieur Van den Besh ... one moment.'

Simon exchanged looks with the secretary. He rose and stepped inside the English-style office which he hated for its perfection.

'Are you aware of the time?'

Maître Fleury launched into a speech extolling

22

punctuality and hard work, rounding it off with a tribute to his own patience and that of Mrs Van den Besh. Simon stared out of the window. It seemed to him that he was reliving a scene from the distant past, that he had always lived in this English-style office, always heard these words; it seemed to him that something was tightening around him, choking him, leading him to his death. What have I done, he suddenly thought, what have I done in twenty-five years but pass from teacher to teacher, forever reprimanded, forever flattered at being so? It was the first time he had put it to himself in such strong terms and he automatically spoke aloud.

'What have I done?'

'Done? But my dear boy, you haven't done a thing. That's just it: you never do.'

'Come to think of it, I've never even loved any-one,' continued Simon.

'I'm not asking you to lose your heart to me or old Alice,' exploded Maître Fleury. 'I'm asking you to work. There are limits to my patience.'

'There are limits to everything,' returned Simon thoughtfully.

He felt entirely adrift, entirely out of touch with the world. As though he had not slept for ten days, as though he were starving, dying of thirst.

'Are you trying to be funny?'

'No,' said Simon. 'Forgive me, I'll pay attention.'

He backed out of the office and sat down at his desk with his head in his hands, under the surprised gaze of Madame Alice. What is the matter with me? he thought. What on earth is the matter with me?

He tried to think back: a childhood in England, universities, a passion – yes, at fifteen – for a friend of his mother's who had initiated him at the end of a week, an easy life, bright friends, girls, roads in the sun . . . everything swirled in his memory, but he could focus on no particular item. Perhaps nothing was the matter. He was twenty-five.

'Don't fret yourself,' said Madame Alice. 'You know he'll get over it.'

He did not answer. He doodled on a blotter.

'Think about your girl friend,' Madame Alice continued anxiously. 'The Guillaut file, rather,' she checked herself.

'I haven't got a girl friend,' said Simon.

'How about the one you met this morning? *What* was her name?'

'I don't know.'

It was true, he did not even know her Christian name. There was someone in Paris he knew nothing about: that in itself was wonderful. Completely unhoped for. Someone he could picture as he wanted for days on end.

*

Roger lay on the divan in the drawing-room; he was smoking slowly, feeling quite worn out. He had spent the day down at the wharf, counting his lorries in; he had been soaked to the skin and, to crown it all, he'd been robbed of his lunch by an accident on the road to Lille which, as he had found on arrival, would cost him over a hundred thousand francs. Paule was clearing the table.

'How about Teresa?' he said.

'Teresa who?'

'Van den Besh. Her Christian name came back to me this morning – God knows why.'

'It's all settled,' said Paule. 'I'm to do the whole flat. I didn't tell you before because you had so many worries . . .'

'Do you think the fact that yours are over would have made me feel worse?'

'No. I just thought . . .'

'Am I so selfish, Paule?'

He had straightened up on the divan and was staring at her out of his blue eyes: he wore his furious look. She was going to have to calm him, to explain to him that he was the best of men – which in a sense was true – and that he made her very happy. She sat down beside him.

'You're not selfish. Your mind is on your work: it's natural you should talk about it . . .'

'No – I mean, in the way I treat you. Do you think I'm very selfish?'

He realized he had been thinking about this all day, probably since he had left her at her door, the night before, with that blurred look in her eyes. She hesitated: he had never asked her before and this might be the time to talk it over with him. But she felt in good form, sure of herself, and he looked so tired . . . She backed down.

'No, Roger. There are times, it's true, when I feel a bit lonely, not so young as I was, unable to keep up with you. But I'm happy.'

'You're happy?'

'Yes.'

He lay back. She had said: 'I'm happy', and now he could rid his mind of the minor disquiet which had dogged him all day. That was all he asked.

'You know, those little flirtations of mine are . . . you don't need me to tell you what they're worth.'

'Of course not,' she said.

She looked at him; she found him childish, lying there with his eyes shut, so tall, so hefty, and asking such puerile questions: 'You're happy?' He reached his hand towards her; she took it and moved closer to him. He kept his eyes shut.

'Paule,' he said. 'Paule . . . Without you, you know, Paule . . .'

'Yes.'

She bent and kissed him on the cheek. He was already asleep. Insensibly he removed his hand from Paule's, lifted it up, and placed it on his heart. She opened a book.

An hour later he woke with great excitement, consulted his watch, and decreed that it was time to go dancing and drinking, so as to forget all those damned lorries. Paule felt sleepy, but no argument could withstand Roger's wants.

He took her somewhere new: a shadowy cellar in the Boulevard Saint-Germain which had been given an outdoor look and was alive with the Latin-American rhythms of a record player.

'I can't go out every night,' said Paule as they sat down. 'I shall feel a hundred tomorrow. This morning was bad enough . . .'

It was only then she remembered Simon. She had entirely forgotten him. She turned to face Roger.

'This morning – can you imagine? – I . . .'

She broke off. Simon was standing in front of her.

'Good evening,' he said.

'Monsieur Ferttet, Monsieur Van den Besh,' said Paule.

'I was looking for you,' said Simon. 'I've found you – it's a good sign.'

And without waiting to be asked, he flopped on to a stool. Roger bridled.

'I've been looking for you everywhere,' Simon continued. 'I was beginning to think you were just a dream.'

His eyes sparkled. He laid his hand on Paule's arm. She was speechless.

'Haven't you a table of your own?' said Roger.

'You're married?' Simon asked Paule. 'I liked to think you weren't.'

'He bores me,' Roger said aloud. 'I'm going to pack him off.'

Simon looked at him, then propped his elbows on the table and put his head in his hands.

'You're right, Monsieur: you must forgive me. I think I've had rather a lot to drink. But I discovered this morning that I had done nothing with my life. Nothing.'

'Then do us a favour and clear off.'

'Let him be,' Paule said gently. 'He's unhappy. We've all had a little too much to drink some time or other. Besides, he's your . . . Teresa's son.'

'He's *what*!' said Roger, with a start. 'Well, I'll be . . .!'

He leaned forward. Simon had sunk his head on to his arms.

'Wake up,' said Roger. 'We'll have a drink together. You can tell us your troubles. I'll go and fetch the drinks: the service is too slow.'

Paule was beginning to have fun. The thought of a conversation between Roger and this young will-o'-the-wisp tickled her. Simon had raised his head; he was watching Roger fight his way between the tables.

'There goes a man,' he said. 'Huh? A real hunk of man? I loathe those beefy, masculine types with their wholesome ideas and their . . .'

'People are never that simple,' Paule said tartly. 'Do you love him?'

'That's no concern of yours.'

A lock of hair hung over his eyes, the candlelight hollowed out his face, he was superb. At the next table, two women surveyed him blissfully.

'Forgive me,' said Simon. 'Gosh, I've done nothing but apologize all day long. I must be pretty uncouth.'

Roger returned with three drinks and growled that it happened to everyone some time or other. Simon drained his glass at a gulp and maintained a discreet silence. He sat beside them and made no move to go. He watched them dance and listened to their talk with such total unresponsiveness that gradually they forgot him. But from time to time Paule would turn and find him sitting at her side like a well-behaved child and she could not help laughing.

When they rose to leave, he stood up politely and collapsed. They decided to take him home. In Roger's car he slept and his head knocked against Paule's shoulder. He had silken hair, he breathed softly. After a time she put her hand to his forehead to stop it hitting the window, and his head grew heavy against her hand; it hung quite loose. When they reached the Avenue Kléber, Roger got out, walked round the front of the car and opened the door.

'Careful,' whispered Paule.

He caught her expression, but said nothing and got Simon out of the car. That night he went up to Paule's flat after driving her back and clutched her to him in his sleep, keeping her awake for hours.

4

At noon next day, as she knelt in the window trying to convince the couturier that as a hat display unit a plaster bust was not quite the last word in originality, Simon arrived. He had been watching her for five minutes, hidden behind a kiosk, with thudding heart. Not knowing any more whether it thudded because he was seeing her or because he was hiding. He had always loved hiding; there were times, too, when he made tortuous use of his left hand, as though the right were clutching a revolver or covered with eczema – this terrified people in shops. It was a case for the psycho-analyst, or so his mother claimed.

As he looked at Paule kneeling in the window, he would have preferred never to have met her; not to be seeing her like this, through the glass. He would not then be faced with the likelihood of a second rebuff. What could he have said the night before? He had behaved like a young fool, got disgustingly drunk, gone on about his moods – the crowning indecency ... He ducked back behind the kiosk, nearly went off, then shot her a final glance. Immediately he wanted to cross the road, snatch the hat away from her – that cruel hat with its long pins – and at the same time snatch *her* away from her work; from this life which got her out of bed at dawn to come and kneel in a shop window in full view of everyone. Passers-by were stopping and gazing at her with curiosity, some of them – no doubt – desiring her as she knelt there, reaching for the plaster bust. He wanted her very much and crossed the road.

He imagined her sick of being stared at, greeting him as a welcome diversion; but she restricted herself to a terse smile.

'Do you want a hat for somebody?'

He started to mumble something, but the couturier hustled him aside, not without coquetry.

'My dear sir, you are waiting for Paule – it's quite all right by me; but sit down over here and let us finish.'

'He isn't waiting for me,' Paule said, shifting a candlestick.

'I'd put it on the left if I were you,' said Simon. 'And a little farther back. It's more evocative.'

For a moment she glared at him. He smiled. Already he had switched parts. Now he was the young man calling for his mistress in elegant surroundings. The young man of exquisite taste. And the admiring sodomite couturier had unsuspectingly become, or was about to become, a standing joke between Paule and himself.

'He's right,' said the couturier. 'It's much more evocative.'

'Of what?' said Paule coldly.

They stared at her.

'Of nothing. Nothing at all.'

And he began to laugh, all to himself, with so gay a laugh that Paule turned away to dissociate herself from it. The couturier withdrew in annoyance. Simon advanced and, as she backed away from the window to get a better view, she knocked his shoulder. His hand closed on her elbow, supporting her on the dais.

'Look,' he said dreamily, 'the sun is out.'

Through the spattered glass the sunlight welled into them with the sudden remorseful warmth of autumn. Paule was aglow with it.

'Yes,' she said, 'the sun is out.'

For a moment they stood quite still, she inches higher on the dais, standing with her back to him yet leaning against him. Then she disengaged herself.

'You should go and sleep.'

'I'm hungry.'

'Then go and eat.'

'You wouldn't care to come with me?'

She hesitated. Roger had telephoned that he would probably be late. She had thought of having a sandwich in the bar across the street and doing some shopping. But this sudden call of the sun made the tiling of the cafés and the aisles of the large stores seem repugnant. She had a craving for grass, even now that it was yellowed by the season.

'I've a craving for grass,' she said.

'Let's go and find some,' he said. 'I have my old car here. The country isn't far . . .'

She flinched. The country with this unknown, possibly boring youngster . . . Two hours *tête-à-tête* . . .

'. . . Or there's the Bois de Boulogne,' he added

reassuringly. 'If you get bored, you can ring for a taxi.'

'You think of everything.'

'I may say I felt pretty ashamed when I woke up. I came to apologize.'

'That kind of thing happens to everyone,' Paule said gently.

She put her coat on. She dressed very well. Simon opened the car door and she took her seat without recalling just when she had said yes to this preposterous lunch. She tore her stocking getting in and gave a small groan of anger.

'I suppose your girl friends wear slacks.'

'I don't have any these days.'

'No girl friends?'

'No.'

'How come?'

'I don't know.'

She wanted to make fun of him. His mixture of timidity and daring, of gravity – at times almost ridiculous – and humour, amused her. The words 'I don't know' had been spoken practically in a whisper and with a great air of mystery. She shook her head.

'Try to remember ... When did this general ostracism begin?'

'It's largely me, you know. I had a girl: she was nice, but too romantic. She was all that men and women of forty imagine young people to be.'

Mentally, she chalked that one up to him.

'How *do* men and women of forty imagine young people?'

'Well . . . She looked sinister; she drove her four c.v. flat out, clenching her teeth; she lit a Gauloise the moment she opened her eyes in the morning . . . and to me she said that love was merely the contact of two skins.'

Paule laughed.

'And . . . ?'

'She still cried when I left her. I'm not proud of that,' he added hurriedly. 'It's a thing I loathe.'

The Bois smelt of wet grass, gently mildewing wood, autumn roads. He pulled up by a small restaurant and tore round the car to open the door for her. Paule made a great muscular effort to get out gracefully. She felt completely on the loose.

Simon at once ordered a cocktail and Paule eyed him sternly.

'After the night you had, you ought to be drinking water.'

'I feel fine. But I need a pick-me-up to stop you from getting too bored.'

The restaurant was practically empty, the waiter sullen. Simon was silent and remained so when they had ordered. Paule, however, was far from being bored. She sensed that this was a deliberate silence, that Simon had planned his conversation for this meal. He must be incessantly full of sly notions, like a cat.

'It's much more evocative,' he simpered suddenly, mimicking the couturier, and Paule, caught off guard, burst out laughing.

'Are you always such a good mimic?'

'Not bad. Unfortunately we don't have many

mutual acquaintances. If I mimic my mother, you'll say I'm contemptible. But here goes: "You don't think a touch of satin just here, a shade to the right, would give a little more warmth and atmosphere?" '

'You're contemptible, but accurate.'

'As for your friend last night, I didn't see him clearly enough. Besides, he must be inimitable.'

There was a momentary silence. Paule smiled.

'He is.'

'Whereas I'm just a pale copy of any number of spoilt young brats, bundled into the professions thanks to their family and filling their time trying to fill their time. It's a come-down for you: this lunch, I mean.'

The aggressiveness of his voice roused Paule.

'Roger was tied up,' she said. 'Otherwise I shouldn't be here.'

'I know,' he said, with a note of sadness which disconcerted her.

For the rest of the meal they spoke of their respective jobs. Simon mimicked a complete hearing of a case of *crime passionnel*. At one point he got to his feet in full spate and levelled a finger at Paule, who was laughing a good deal.

'As for you, I accuse you of failing in your duty as a human being. In the name of the deceased, I accuse you of letting love go by, of neglecting your duty to be happy, of living on evasion, subterfuge, and resignation. You ought to be sentenced to death, you *will* be sentenced to loneliness.'

He stopped and drained his glass at a gulp. Paule had not batted an eyelid.

'A stiff sentence,' she said with a smile.

'The worst,' he said. 'I can think of nothing worse, nor more inevitable. It frightens me more than anything else. It frightens everyone. But no one will admit it. There are times when I want to shout it from the roof-tops: "I'm frightened, I'm frightened – love me!"'

'Me too,' she said, as though involuntarily.

In a flash she saw the wall beyond the foot of her bed. With the drawn curtains, the unfashionable picture, the little chest of drawers on the left. The view which daily confronted her, night and morning, which would probably still confront her in ten years' time. When she was even lonelier than she was today. What was Roger playing at? He had no right, nobody could condemn her to get old like this; nobody, not even herself . . .

'I must strike you as even more ridiculous and whimpering than last night,' said Simon softly. 'Or perhaps you think it's just a boyish trick to get round you?'

He sat facing her, his pale eyes rather bleary, his face so smooth and open that she nearly put her hand to it.

'No, no,' she said, 'I was thinking . . . I was also thinking that you were a bit young for that. And certainly too well loved.'

'One can't live alone,' he said. 'Come on, we'll stretch our legs. It's beautiful out now.'

They went out together, he took her arm and they walked for a while, without a word. Autumn welled up in Paule's heart, with great sweetness.

The damp, russet leaves, clinging and trampled on, merged slowly on the ground. She felt a kind of fondness for the silent figure holding her arm. For a few minutes this stranger became a companion, someone to walk with, down a deserted avenue, at the year's close. She had always experienced fondness for her male companions, whether she took walks with them or lived with them, a kind of gratitude to them for being taller than she, at once so different and so like. Into her mind came the face of Marc, the husband she had left at the same time as the easy life; the face of another who had greatly loved her. And finally Roger's face, the only face her memory projected live, with changes of expression. Three companions in one woman's lifetime, three good companions. Wasn't that after all considerable?

'Are you feeling sad?' asked Simon.

She turned to him and smiled without answering. They kept walking.

'I should like,' said Simon in a strangled voice, 'I should like ... I don't know you, but I should like to think you were happy. I – er, I admire you.'

She had stopped listening to him. It was late. Roger might have rung to suggest coffee. She would have missed him. He had talked of leaving on Saturday and spending the week-end in the country. Would she be able to get through her work in time? Would he still want to go? Or was this another of those promises which love and night-time wrenched from him, when (as she knew) he no longer envisaged life without her and their love struck him as so self-evident that he no longer struggled? But the moment he left the flat, the moment – outside on the pavement – he inhaled the heady aroma of his independence, she lost him again. She said little during the ride back, thanked Simon for giving her lunch, and swore she would be delighted if he rang her one of these days. Simon watched her walk away. He did not move. He felt gauche and very weary.

5

I⊤ really was a pleasant surprise. Roger turned to the bedside table and rummaged for a cigarette. The young woman beside him gave a short laugh.

'Men always smoke, afterwards.'

It was not a very original reflection! Roger held the packet out to her. She shook her head.

'Maisy, may I ask you a question? What's got into you tonight? Two months we've known each other, and you've never left Monsieur Chérel's side . . .'

'Monsieur Chérel is useful for my work. I felt like having fun. Understand, my honey?'

He noted in passing that she was one of those women who became possessive the moment they lay on their backs. He laughed.

'But why me? There were some good-looking youngsters at the party.'

'Oh, the young ones talk and talk. At least you look as though you know what you want. And that's getting to be rare, believe you me. It's a thing women can sense. Don't tell me you're not used to making a hit . . .'

'Not quite so soon,' he laughed.

She was very pretty. No doubt her cribbed brain was teeming with petty notions about life, men, women. Given the slightest encouragement, she would tell him what made the world go round. He would have loved that. As always he felt remote yet touched, appalled by the thought of these beautiful bodies, all so different and so splendid to explore, wandering through the streets and through life guided by small, wavering, restricted heads. He stroked her hair.

'I bet you're an old softy,' she said. 'Great brutes like you always are.'

'Of course,' he said, absent-mindedly.

'I don't feel like leaving you,' she went on. 'If only you knew what a bore Chérel is . . .'

'I never shall.'

'Suppose we went away for a couple of days, Roger? Saturday and Sunday. Wouldn't you like that? We'd put up at a country inn and not stir from our room all day.'

He looked at her. She had propped herself up on one elbow; he saw the pulse racing in her neck; she was looking at him just as she had in the course of that precious party; he smiled.

'Say yes. Right this minute, do you hear me?'

'Right this minute,' he repeated, drawing her to him.

She bit his shoulder and gurgled, and it crossed his mind that even love could be made stupidly.

*

'What a shame,' said Paule. 'Anyway, work well and don't drive too fast. All my love.'

She hung up. That was the end of their week-end. Roger had to go to Lille on Saturday, he had explained, to do business with his associate there. It might be true. She always supposed it was true. Suddenly she thought of the inn where they generally went together, of the fires blazing everywhere, of the bedroom smelling slightly of mothballs; she imagined what those two days might have been, the walks with Roger, the conversations with Roger in the evening, the awakenings at each other's side, with time stretching before them, a whole day, warm and smooth as a beach. She turned back to the telephone. She could lunch with a friend, have an evening's bridge with ... There was nothing she wanted to do. And she dreaded being alone for two days. She hated these spinster Sundays: staying in bed with a book for as long as she could; a crowded cinema; perhaps drinks with someone, or a dinner; and finally coming home to this unmade bed, feeling that she had not been even momentarily alive since morning. Roger had said he would ring her next day. He had spoken with his loving voice. She would wait in for his call. In any case, she had some tidying to do – some of those humdrum jobs which her mother had always prescribed, those myriad trifles of a woman's life which vaguely disgusted her. As though time had been a flabby beast which needed fining down. But she had come almost to regret her lack of this impulse. Perhaps a moment really came when one no longer had to attack one's life, but to defend oneself from it as from some old and tactless friend. Had it come already? And at her back she thought she heard an immense sigh, an immense chorus of 'Already ...'

At two o'clock on that same Saturday, she decided

to ring Mrs Van den Besh. If, by some miracle, she weren't at Deauville, she might be able to spend the afternoon working with her. It was the only thing that appealed to her. Like those men, she thought, who go to the office on Sundays to avoid their families. Mrs Van den Besh was having slight trouble with her liver, sounded distinctly bored, and greeted her proposal with enthusiasm. She found Mrs Van den Besh in a damask dressing-gown, a glass of mineral water in her hand, looking slightly blotchy. Paule momentarily reflected that Simon's father must have been very handsome to offset the banality of her face.

'How is your son? You know we ran into him the other evening.'

She did not add that she had lunched with him only the day before; she was amazed at her own reticence. At once she met with a martyred expression.

'How *should* I know? He doesn't talk to me; he doesn't tell me about anything – except his money troubles, of course! What's more, he drinks. His father drank too, you know.'

'He hardly looks a dipsomaniac,' smiled Paule. She thought of Simon's smooth face and flourishing English complexion.

'He's handsome, isn't he?'

Mrs Van den Besh grew animated and produced albums portraying Simon as a child, Simon on a pony with ringlets flowing down his cheeks, Simon as a gaping schoolboy, etc. There were, no doubt, a thousand photographs of him and Paule secretly marvelled that he had become neither odious, nor a sodomite.

'But there always comes a time when children grow away from you,' sighed the aggrieved mother.

And a moment later she became the rather flighty woman she must once have been.

'I may say there's no lack of opportunities . . .'

'I'm sure,' said Paule politely. 'Would you like to look at these fabrics, Madame? There is one here that . . .'

'Do call me Teresa.'

She grew friendly, rang for tea, asked questions. Paule reflected that Roger had slept with her twenty years before, and searched her doughy face in vain for some remnant of charm. At the same time, she tried desperately to keep the conversation on a professional footing, but watched Teresa sink inexorably into womanly confidences. It was always the same. There was something fine and stable about her face which unleashed the deadliest torrents of words.

'You are probably younger than I,' began Mrs Van den Besh (and Paule could not suppress a smile at the 'probably'), 'but you know what a difference surroundings can make . . .'

Paule had stopped listening to her. The woman reminded her of someone. She realized that she merely bore out the imitation Simon had given the day before; he must, she thought, have a certain intuitive faculty, a certain cruelty which was obscured by his shyness. What was it he had said? *I accuse you of letting love go by, of living on subterfuge and resignation: I sentence you to loneliness.* Had he meant her? Had he divined something of her life? Had he said it on purpose? She felt a wave of anger at the thought.

She had stopped listening to the ceaseless chatter at her side, and Simon's entrance made her jump. He stopped short at the sight of her and pulled a face to mask his pleasure. She was touched.

'I picked the right time to come in. I'll give you a hand.'

'Alas, I must be going.'

She felt like rushing out, taking to her heels, escaping from the stares of mother and son, hiding herself at home with a book. At this hour she should have been on the road with Roger, flicking the radio on and off, laughing with him or quailing – for as a driver he was prone to blind rages which sometimes brought them close to death. She got slowly to her feet.

'I'll see you out,' said Simon.

At the door she turned and looked at him for the first time since his arrival. He looked out of sorts and she could not help saying so.

'It's the weather,' he said. 'May I come down with you?'

She shrugged and they started down the stairs. He walked behind her, without a word. On the final landing he stopped, and she turned automatically, no longer hearing his tread. He was leaning against the banister.

'Are you going back?'

The light went out and the huge staircase was left with only a faint glimmer from a casement window. Her eyes searched for the time-switch.

'It's behind you,' said Simon.

He cleared the last flight and came towards her. He's going to grab me, thought Paule with annoyance. He reached his left arm past her head and switched on; then he set his right arm on the other side of her. She could not move.

'Let me pass,' she said, very calmly.

He did not answer, but stooped down and cautiously rested his head on her shoulder. She heard her heart thudding away and suddenly felt perturbed.

'Let me pass, Simon . . . You're annoying me.'

But he did not move. All he did was softly murmur her name twice – 'Paule, Paule' – and beyond the back of his head she saw the well of the stairs, so dreary, so oppressively silent and gloomy.

'*Mon petit Simon*,' she said, just as softly, 'let me pass.'

He drew back and she smiled at him for a moment before going out into the street.

6

SHE woke on Sunday to find a note under her door
that would once have been poetically known as a
bleu; today she found it poetic because the sun, re-
appearing in the flawless November sky, filled her
room with shadows and warm patches of light.
'There is a wonderful concert in the Salle Pleyel at
six,' Simon wrote. '*Aimez-vous Brahms?* I'm sorry
about yesterday.' She smiled. She smiled on account
of the second sentence: *Aimez-vous Brahms?* It was
one of these questions young men had asked her
when she was seventeen. And no doubt she had been
asked the same things later, but with no one
listening to the answer. In that set, and at that time
of life, who listened to whom? Come to think of it:
did she care for Brahms?

She opened the lid of her record-player, poked
about among her records and found, on the back of
a Wagner overture she knew by heart, a Brahms
concerto she had never listened to. Roger loved
Wagner. 'It's beautiful,' he would say, 'it makes a
noise, it's music.' She put the concerto on, found
the beginning romantic and forgot to listen to all of
it. She awoke to the fact when the music stopped and
was angry with herself. Nowadays she took six days
to read a book, lost her place, forgot music. She
could not keep her mind on a thing, except fabric
samples and a man who was never there. She was

losing herself, losing track of herself; she would never be herself again. *Aimez-vous Brahms?* For a moment she stood by the open window; the sunlight hit her full in the eyes and dazzled her. And this little phrase, *Aimez-vous Brahms*, seemed suddenly to reveal an enormous forgetfulness: all that she had forgotten, all the questions that she had deliberately refrained from asking herself. *Aimez-vous Brahms?* Did she care for anything, now, except herself and her own existence? Of course, she said she loved Stendhal; she knew she loved him. That was the word: knew. Perhaps she merely 'knew' she loved Roger. Sound acquisitions. Sound touchstones. She felt an itch to talk to someone, as she had felt at twenty.

She rang Simon. She did not yet know what to say to him. Probably: 'I don't know whether I care for Brahms. I don't think so.' She did not know whether she would go to the concert. It would depend on what he said to her, on his tone of voice; she was hesitant and found this hesitancy delightful. But Simon had gone out into the country for lunch, he would be back at five to change his clothes. She hung up. Meanwhile she had decided to go to the concert. She told herself: 'It isn't Simon I'm going for, but the music. Perhaps I'll go every Sunday evening if the atmosphere isn't too awful: it's just the thing for a single woman to do.' And at the same time she regretted that it was Sunday and she couldn't rush out to the shops and buy the Mozarts she loved and a few Brahms. Her only fear was that Simon might hold her hand during the concert;

this she feared especially because she was expecting it, and the confirmation of her expectations always bored her beyond words. She had loved Roger for that, too. He always side-stepped the obvious, giving a certain twist to the most humdrum situations.

At six o'clock in the Salle Pleyel she was caught in the press of late-comers and nearly missed Simon, who silently handed her a ticket; they tore upstairs amid a flurry of attendants. The hall was huge and shadowy, and the orchestra produced a few particularly discordant sounds by way of pre-amble, as though to make the audience more appreciative of the miracle of musical harmony. She turned to her companion.

'I didn't know whether I cared for Brahms.'

'And *I* didn't know whether you'd come,' said Simon. 'I assure you I'm not bothered whether you care for Brahms or not.'

'How was the country?'

He looked at her in astonishment.

'I rang you,' said Paule, 'to say that . . . that I should be glad to come.'

'I was so afraid you would say the opposite, or not ring at all, that I went out,' said Simon.

'Was the country looking lovely? Whereabouts did you go?'

It gave her a sad feeling of pleasure to imagine Houdan hill in the evening light; she would have loved Simon to talk about it. By this time she would have stopped in Septeuil with Roger, they would have followed the same track beneath the russet trees.

'Oh, here and there,' said Simon, 'I didn't look at the names. Anyway, the concert is starting.'

There was applause, the conductor bowed, he raised his baton and they settled into their seats at the same time as two thousand others. It was a concerto which Simon thought he recognized, a trifle sentimental, a trifle too sentimental at times. He felt Paule's elbow against his and when the orchestra soared, he soared with it. But as soon as the music flagged he grew conscious of their neighbours' coughing, of the shape of a man's head two rows in front, and – most of all – conscious of his anger. In the country, at an inn near Houdan, he had met Roger – Roger with a girl. He had stood up and greeted Simon, without introducing him.

'We always seem to be running into each other.'

Simon had been too taken aback to say anything. Roger's stare was threatening him, ordering him to keep mum about this meeting: it was not, thank God, the conniving stare of one gay dog to another. It was a furious stare. He had not answered. He was not afraid of Roger, he was afraid of hurting Paule; for the first time he wanted to interpose between someone and distress. He of all people – normally so quick to tire of his mistresses; so terrified of their confidences, their secrets, their relentless desire for him to play the protective male; so prone to flight – now wanted to turn and wait. But wait for what? For this woman to realize that she was in love with a heel? There was, perhaps, no slower process ... She must be feeling sad, turning Roger's attitude over in her mind, maybe discovering its faults. A violin soared above the orchestra, throbbed desperately on a shattered note and fell back, to be drowned at once in the encroaching flood of melody. Simon nearly turned, took Paule in his arms, and kissed her. Yes, kissed her . . . He imagined that he was leaning over her, that his mouth was against hers, that she was drawing his hands around her neck . . . He shut his eyes. Paule thought, from his expression, that he must be really mad on music. But at once a trembling hand groped for hers and she freed herself impatiently.

After the concert he took her out for a drink, which meant an orange squash for her and a double gin for him. She wondered if Mrs Van den Besh's fears were justified. Simon – eyes shining, hands fluttering – was talking music and she listened abstractedly. Roger might have contrived to get back from Lille in time for dinner. Besides, people were looking at them. Simon was a little too good-looking; or was he merely a little too young, and she not quite young enough – for him, at least ?

'Aren't you listening ?'

'Yes,' she said. 'But we ought to be going. I'm expecting a phone call, and people are staring at us.'

'You ought to be used to that,' said Simon admiringly. What with the music and the gin, he was feeling distinctly amorous.

She laughed: at times he was altogether disarming.

'Ask for the bill, Simon.'

He asked for it with such reluctance that she

looked at him closely, probably for the first time that evening. Perhaps he was falling quietly in love with her, perhaps he had been hoist with his own petard? She had thought him merely athirst for conquests; perhaps he was more straightforward, more sensitive, less vain. Odd that it should be his looks which set her against him. She found him too handsome. Too handsome to be true.

If that were the case, she was wrong to see him, she should put a stop to it. He had called the waiter and was twirling his glass between his hands, without a word. He had suddenly lost his tongue. She laid her hand on his.

'Don't be angry with me, Simon, I'm in rather a hurry. Roger must be waiting for me.'

He had asked her, that first evening, in the Saint-Germain cellar: 'Do you love Roger?' What had she said? She could not remember. At all events, he had to know.

'Oh yes,' he said. 'Roger. The man. The brilliant . . .'

She stopped him.

'I love him,' she said, and she felt herself blush. She had the impression that she had spoken theatrically.

'And him?'

'Him too.'

'Naturally. All is for the best in the best of all possible worlds.'

'Don't act the cynic,' she said gently. 'It doesn't go with your years. At your age you ought to believe these things, you . . .'

He had seized her by the shoulders and was shaking her.

'Don't make fun of me. Stop talking like that . . .'

I'm too inclined to forget he is a man, thought Paule, trying to free herself. He looks a man now, right enough: a man who's been humiliated. It's true: he's twenty-five, not fifteen.

'It's not you I'm making fun of, but your attitudes,' she said gently. 'You're acting a part.'

He had released her. He seemed tired.

'It's true,' he said. 'With you I've acted the young and brilliant lawyer, and the bashful lover, and the spoilt child, and heaven knows what. But since I've known you, all my roles have been for you. Don't you think that's love?'

'It's rather a good definition,' she said with a smile.

They were silent for a few moments, equally embarrassed.

'I wish we could act the part of passionate lovers,' he said.

'I've told you: I love Roger.'

'And I love my mother, my old nurse, my car . . .'

'I don't see the connexion,' she broke in.

She wanted to leave. What could this voracious boy know of her affair, their affair, of these five years of mingled pleasure and doubt, warmth and pain? Nobody could come between her and Roger. She so warmed to Simon for convincing her that, instead of going, she rested her elbows on the table.

'You love Roger but you are alone,' said Simon.

'You spend your Sundays alone, you dine alone and probably you ... you often sleep alone. I'd sleep beside you, I'd hold you in my arms all night and I'd kiss you while you were asleep. I still know what it is to love. He doesn't. You know he doesn't ...'

'You've no right ...' she said, rising to her feet.

'I have the right to speak. I have the right to fall in love with you and take you away from him, if I can.'

Already she was out in the street. He rose, then sat down again, his head in his hands. I must have her, he thought, I must have her ... or I shall suffer.

7

THE week-end had been very agreeable. The girl
Maisy – she had confessed, with a smirk, to having
been christened plain Marcelle, a name for obvious
reasons incompatible with her vocation as a starlet –
the girl Maisy had kept her word. Once in bed, she
had stayed there, unlike certain creatures of Roger's
acquaintance who fussed about cocktail-time and
lunch-time and dinner-time and tea-time and so
forth; just so many excuses for a change of costume.
They had gone two days without leaving their
room, except once, when naturally he had run into
that young milksop, dear Teresa's son. He was un-
likely to be seeing Paule, of course, but Roger was
left feeling vaguely uneasy. The Lille story had
been a little thin, not that he imagined he deluded
Paule with his infidelities, or even his lies. But his
lapses ought not to be pinned down to a particular
place or time. 'I saw your friend from the other
evening. He was having lunch in Houdan on
Sunday.' He pictured Paule hearing the news and
saying nothing, perhaps turning her head away for
a moment. Paule suffering . . . It was an old picture
by now, and one so often brushed aside that he was
ashamed of it, as he was ashamed of the pleasure he
would derive from calling on her within the next
few minutes, after dropping Maisy-Marcelle. But
she wouldn't know. She must have spent the two

days resting, without him there to keep her out late; she must have been playing bridge with her friends, working about the flat, reading that new book . . . Suddenly he wondered why he was striving so hard to hit upon something that Paule might do with her Sundays.

'You drive well,' said a voice beside him. He came to with a start and looked at Maisy.

'Think so?'

'Come to that, you do everything well,' she continued, lolling in her seat.

And he longed to tell her to forget: to forget her little body and her satisfied appetites for a moment. She gave a languorous, or would-be languorous, laugh and taking his hand laid it on her thigh. The thigh was hard and warm beneath his fingers, and he smiled. She was foolish, prating, and affected. She made such a mockery of love that it became curiously down to earth, and her way of shattering any desire he might have for tenderness, comradeship, or even faint interest made her more exciting. A dirty little thing; dumb, pretentious, vulgar; someone with whom he made love well. He laughed aloud. She did not ask why, but reached for the radio. Roger followed the movement with his eyes . . . What was it Paule had said the other night? About the radio and their evenings out . . . ? He could not remember. A concert was on the air; she dialled away from it, then returned to it for lack of anything better. ' . . . by Brahms,' said the announcer in a quavering voice, and there was a crackle of applause.

'When I was eight, I wanted to be a conductor,' he said. 'And you?'

'I wanted to be in films,' she said, 'and one day I shall be.'

He thought it was probable and finally dropped her at her door. She clung to his jacket.

'Tomorrow I'm having dinner with that awful man Chérel. But I want to see my little Roger again very, very soon. I'll ring you the first chance I get.'

He smiled, rather pleased with the role of the young lover in hiding, especially from a man of his own age.

'What about you?' she pursued. 'Can you manage it? I was told you weren't a free agent . . .'

'I'm a free agent,' he said with a slight grimace. He certainly didn't intend to discuss Paule with her! She gambolled over the pavement, waved from the porchway, and he drove off. His last remark slightly troubled him. 'I'm a free agent.' That meant: free not to take on responsibilities. He accelerated: he wanted to see Paule again as soon as possible; she alone could reassure him, and she would.

*

She must have got back just before him, for she still had her coat on; she was pale, and when he arrived she flung herself at him and hung against his shoulder, without stirring. He folded his arms about her, rested his cheek on her hair and waited for her to speak. He had been right to hurry back; she needed him; something must have happened to her; and, as he reflected on how he had known it in his bones, he felt his fondness for her become intense. He protected her. Of course, she was strong, and independent, and intelligent, but she was probably more female than any woman he had ever known, as he was well aware. And to that extent he was indispensable to her. She gently freed herself from his arms.

'Did you have a good journey? How was Lille?'

He shot a glance at her. No, of course she suspected nothing. She was not the kind of woman to set traps like that. He raised his eyebrows.

'So-so. But you? What's wrong?'

'Nothing,' she said, and she turned away.

He did not press the matter; she would tell him later.

'What have you been up to?'

'Yesterday I worked. And today I went to a concert at the Pleyel.'

'*Aimez-vous Brahms?*' he said with a smile.

She had her back to him, and she swung round so abruptly that he recoiled.

'Why do you ask?'

'I heard part of the concert on the radio, on the way back.'

'Yes, of course,' she said, 'I'd forgotten it was broadcast . . . But you surprised me: it isn't like you to be so musical.'

'Nor you. What came over you? I imagined you playing bridge at the Darets or . . .'

She had turned on the sitting-room lights. She wearily took off her coat.

'Young Van den Besh invited me to the concert; I had nothing to do, and I couldn't remember whether I cared for Brahms . . . Can you imagine? . . . I couldn't remember whether I cared for Brahms . . .'

She began to laugh, softly at first, then more and more loudly. Roger's brain was in a whirl. Simon Van den Besh? And he had not spoken of their meeting . . . in Houdan? Why was she laughing, anyway?

'Paule,' he said, 'calm down. What were you doing with that popinjay, anyway?'

'I was listening to Brahms,' she said between laughs.

'Do stop talking about Brahms . . .'

'I can hardly leave him out . . .'

He seized her by the shoulders. She had tears in her eyes from laughing so much.

'Paule,' he said, 'my Paule . . . what has that character been telling you? And what does he want out of you, anyway?'

He was furious; he felt outdistanced and derided.

'He's twenty-five, of course,' he said.

'To me that's a failing,' she said tenderly, and he took her in his arms again.

'Paule, I trust you so much. So very much! I can't stand the thought of your falling for a young cub like that.'

He hugged her to him; suddenly he imagined Paule reaching out for someone else, Paule kissing someone else, giving her fondness and attention to someone else; he was in pain.

Paule thought without bitterness: men really are amazing. 'I trust you so much' – so much that I can deceive you and abandon you, yet there can be no question of the same thing happening in reverse.

It took one's breath away.

'He's nice and he's unimportant,' she said. 'That's all there is to it. Where do you want us to eat?'

8

'Forgive me,' wrote Simon. 'It's true: I had no right to say that. I was jealous, and I suppose one has the right to be jealous only of what one possesses. Anyway, it seems clear I was rather boring you. Well, now you are rid of me. I'm leaving town, to work on a case with my chief, bless him. We shall be living in an old country house belonging to friends of his. I imagine the beds will smell of verbena, there will be a fire in every room, and the birds will sing outside my window in the mornings. But I know that for once in my life I shall be unable to act the young rustic. You will sleep beside me; I shall picture you in reach, by the light of the flames; I shall be within an ace of returning a dozen times. Do not think – even if you never want to see me again – do not think I don't love you. Your Simon.'

The letter faltered in Paule's grasp. It slipped on to the sheet, then on to the carpet. Paule laid her head back on the pillow and shut her eyes. No doubt he loved her . . . She was tired this morning, she had slept badly. Was it because of the brief sentence Roger had let slip the night before, when she had asked him about his return journey? She had not at once caught on to it, but he had stumbled over it and his voice had dropped almost to a murmur.

'Of course, it's always dreadful driving back on

Sundays ... But at least the motorway is quick, even when it's crowded ...'

Had he not changed his tone, she would doubtless not have noticed it. She would have immediately imagined – thanks to an unconscious mental reflex, that terrible, self-protective reflex which had grown so over the past two years – she would have imagined a wonderful, brand new motorway to Lille. But he had broken off, she had not looked at him, and it had been left to her, fifteen seconds later, to steer their talk back on to its unruffled path. Their dinner had ended on the same note, but it seemed to Paule that the tiredness and dejection she felt, far more than any jealousy or curiosity, would never leave her. Across the table his face was taut: that loved, familiar face, scanning hers to discover whether she had realized, scanning it for signs of suffering, as though they would cause him intolerable pain. At this she thought: isn't it enough for him to make me suffer; does he *have* to care about it? And it seemed to her that she would never be able to rise from her chair and cross the restaurant with the ease and grace which he expected of her, or even to bid him *au revoir* at her doorstep. She would have loved to behave differently: she would have loved to insult him, to fling her glass at him, to forget herself, forget everything that made her seem fine and up-standing, everything that distinguished her from the pack of sluts he went around with. She would have loved to be one of them. He had told her often enough how little they meant to him, that he was like that and had no wish to hide it from her. Yes, he had been honest. But she wondered whether honesty, the only honesty possible in this inextricable life, did not consist in loving someone enough to make her happy. Even if it meant being less self-indulgent.

Simon's letter still lay on the carpet and she trod on it getting out of bed. She picked it up and read it again. Then she opened the drawer of her desk, took out pen and paper, and replied.

*

Simon had hung back in the drawing-room, not wishing to mingle with the crowd congratulating the Grand Maître on the outcome of the case. The house was cold and dismal. There had been a frost in the night and the window revealed a captive landscape, two bare trees, and a moribund lawn where a pair of rattan seats were quietly rotting, sacrificed to autumn by a neglectful gardener. Simon was reading an English book, a strange story about a woman who turned into a fox, and from time to time he laughed aloud. But his legs would not keep still; he crossed them, then uncrossed them, and gradually his feeling of malaise came between him and the book until finally he rose, set the book down, and went out.

He walked as far as a small pond at the foot of the garden, inhaling the smell of coldness and the smell of evening, to which was added the more distant smell of burning leaves: he could barely distinguish the smoke behind a hedge. He liked this final smell more than anything and momentarily halted and closed his eyes, so that he could really take it in. Occasionally a bird would give a small, graceless cry, and the perfect unity and cohesion of its yearnings dimly consoled him in his own. He bent over the murky water, plunged his hand in, and stared at his lean fingers to which the water gave the appearance of sloping almost perpendicularly from the palm. He did not move, but closed his hand in the water, slowly, as though to capture some mysterious fish. He had not seen Paule in seven days now, seven and a half days. She must have received his letter, given a slight shrug, and hidden it so that Roger should not find it and make fun of him. For she was kind, as he well knew. She was kind and affectionate and unhappy, and he needed her. But how was he to let her know? He had already tried, one evening in this sinister house, tried to think of her so long and so intensely that he would get through to her in her far-off Paris, and had even come down in his pyjamas to scour the library for a work on telepathy. In vain, of course! He knew it was puerile: he always tried to get out of things by childish solutions or strokes of luck. But Paule was someone you had to deserve, there was no escaping the fact. He could not win her merely by charm. On the contrary, he felt that his looks set her against him. 'I've a face like a hairdresser's assistant,' he groaned aloud, and the bird momentarily broke off its piercing cry.

He walked slowly back to the house, stretched out on the carpet, put another log on the fire. Maître Fleury would be back soon, modest in his triumph but even more sure of himself than usual. He would revive famous trials before a few dazzled countrywomen who, their brains tiring slightly towards the end of the meal and their eyes somewhat blurred with wine, would begin to transfer their attentions to the young, silent, well-mannered pupil – to himself, in fact. 'You stand a chance with that one, young Simon,' Maître Fleury would whisper, probably singling out the oldest. They had been away together before, but the obsessive allusions of the great advocate had never led either of them into much mischief.

His anticipations were borne out. Only, it was one of the gayest dinners in his life: he talked endlessly, broke in upon the great advocate, and captivated every woman in the room. On arrival, Maître Fleury had handed him a letter which had been forwarded from the Avenue Kléber to the Palais de Justice in Rouen. It was from Paule. He put his hand in his pocket, felt it against his fingers, and smiled with happiness. And even as he talked, he tried to recall its exact wording, quietly reconstructing it in his head.

'*Mon petit Simon*' – she had always called him that – 'your letter was too sad. It is more than I deserve. Besides, I was missing you. I'm none too clear where I stand at the moment' – and then she had written his name again: 'Simon,' and then she had added those three wonderful words: 'Come back soon.'

He was going back at once, the moment dinner was over. He would drive flat out for Paris, he would stop in front of her house, perhaps he would see her.

At two o'clock he was there, unable to budge. Half an hour later a car drew up in front of him and Paule got out, alone. He did not budge. He watched her cross the road and wave at the car, which drove off. He could not budge. It was Paule. He loved her and he listened to the love within him call out to her, go up to her, speak to her: he listened without budging, terrified, his mind aching and empty.

9

THE lake in the Bois de Boulogne stretched icily
before them under a cheerless sun; a hardy oarsman – one of those strange men one daily sees trying
to preserve a figure which no one could possibly care
about, so characterless is their appearance – was
making a lone effort to resurrect the summer, his
oar sending up an occasional spray of water, silvery,
sparkling, and almost inopportune, so sadly did
winter proclaim itself among the frozen shapes of
the trees. She watched him tussling down in the
boat, his brow puckered with determination. He
would row round the island and come back exhausted and pleased with himself: she found a touch
of symbolism in this short, obdurate, daily pull.
Simon, beside her, was silent. He was waiting. She
turned to him and smiled. He looked at her without
returning her smile. The Paule for whom he had
driven right across a province the night before (a
Paule not merely available but naked and van-
quished in his mind like the road he had driven
along) had nothing in common with the tranquil
Paule (she had been barely pleased to see him) who
drowsed beside him on an iron bench in trite surroundings. He was disappointed and, misinter-
preting his disappointment, he thought he did not
love her any more. That obsessed week in the
country, in that dreary house, had been a perfect

example of the absurdities into which his imagination could lead him. Yet he could not repress this aching desire within him, this dizziness at the very thought of tilting her weary head against the back of the bench, thereby bruising the nape of her neck, and of lowering his lips on to those serene full lips from which had flowed, for two hours now, a stream of gracious, pacifying words which he had no wish to hear. She had written: 'Come back soon.' And more than his longing for these words he rued his delight at receiving them, his ridiculous feeling of joy, his confidence. He preferred having been unhappy for a worthwhile reason to being happy for a poor one. He told her so, and her eyes swung away from the oarsman to settle on him.

'*Mon petit Simon*, everyone feels that way: it's perfectly natural.'

She laughed. He had arrived at her flat like a madman that morning, and she had at once made it clear to him that her letter did not mean a thing.

'All the same,' he resumed, 'you're not a woman who would write "Come back soon" to absolutely anyone.'

'I was lonely,' she said. 'And in a funny mood. Of course, you're right: I shouldn't have written "Come back soon".'

Yet she was thinking the opposite. He was there, and she was happy he was there. So lonely! She had been so lonely! Roger was having another affair (she had not been allowed to overlook it) with a film-struck blonde; he seemed rather ashamed, although they never discussed it, but his alibis revealed an

67

ingenuity which contentment did not normally prompt in him. She had dined with him twice that week. Only twice. In fact, had it not been for this young man beside her, unhappy thanks to her, she would have been extremely unhappy herself.

'Come on,' he said, 'let's get back. You're bored.'

She rose unprotestingly. She felt like driving him to breaking-point and reproached herself, as with an act of cruelty. It was the reverse side of her sadness, this cruelty: an absurd need to exact undeserved revenge from him. They got into Simon's tiny car, and he gave a bitter smile at the thought of how this first outing together ought to have gone: he should have been driving left-handed with prodigious skill, his right hand lodged in Paule's and that beautiful head resting on his shoulder. He reached his hand blindly towards her and she took it in both hers. She thought: shall I never, never be able to play the fool? He stopped the car; she said nothing, and he looked at his hand, lying limp in Paule's; hers were slightly parted, ready to let his escape (which was probably all they were waiting for), and he threw back his head, suddenly sick to death, resigned to leaving her for good. In that moment he had aged thirty years, he had submitted to life, and it seemed to Paule that she knew him for the first time.

For the first time he struck her as being like her, like them (herself and Roger). Not vulnerable, for she had always known he was that, and she could not imagine anyone who wasn't. But freed, stripped of everything that his youth, beauty, and inexperience had damned in her eyes; somehow or other, she had always seen him as a prisoner – a prisoner of his facility, the facility of his life. And now he sat there, proffering – not to her, but to the trees – that dying profile, the face of a man who has given up the struggle. Simultaneously she recalled the gay, bewildered Simon she had met in his dressing-gown, and she wanted to restore him to his old self, to send him away for good, thereby consigning him to a momentary grief and a thousand future, all too predictable young women. Time would instruct him better, and less hastily, than she. He let his hand lie limply in hers, she felt his pulse against her fingers and suddenly, with tears in her eyes, not knowing whether she shed them for this susceptible young man or for her own rather dreary life, she carried the hand to her lips and kissed it.

He said nothing, but let in the clutch. For the first time, something had occurred between them; he knew it and he was even happier than the night before. She had finally 'seen' him, and if he had been fool enough to suppose that the first occurrence between them could only be a night of love, he had no one but himself to blame. He was going to need a lot of patience, a lot of tenderness, and, no doubt, a lot of time. And he felt patient, tender, with the whole of life ahead of him. Indeed, he thought that this night of love, if it came, would be merely a stage and not the culmination to which he generally looked forward: there would be days and nights between them, perhaps, but it would never be finished. At the same time, he desired her fiercely.

IO

MRS VAN DEN BESH was getting old. Having always had up to then – on account of her looks and what one might almost have called, certainly until that unhoped-for marriage with Jerome Van den Besh, a 'vocation' – more men friends than women, she experienced with the onset of age a loneliness which threw her out of gear and flung her at the first person who came along, male or female. She found Paule's company ideal, purely on the strength of their business relationship. The flat in the Avenue Kléber was upside-down: Paule had to call there practically every day and Mrs Van den Besh invented countless excuses for detaining her. Besides, for all her apparent wool-gathering, Paule seemed to be very friendly with Simon, and although Mrs Van den Besh had failed to uncover the smallest trace of any more definite bond between them she could not help treating her to winks and allusions that seemed lost on Paule but drove Simon out of his mind. Which was how, pale and distraught, he came to grab hold of her one evening and threaten her – *her*, his mother! – with terrible violence if she went and 'spoiled' everything.

'Spoil what? Will you let go of me? Do you sleep with her or don't you?'

'I've already told you I don't.'

'Well then . . . If it isn't already in her mind, I

put it there. You ought to thank your lucky stars. She's not a child. You take her to concerts and round the galleries and heaven knows where . . . Do you think that's what she wants? Why you numskull, you don't realize . . .'

But Simon was already out of the flat. He had been back three weeks now and lived by Paule and for Paule and on the few hours she sometimes accorded him during the day, leaving her only at the last minute and holding her hand in his for a moment too long, like the romantic heroes he had always derided. So he was horrified when, the day her drawing-room was finished, his mother decided to give a dinner and invite Paule. She added that she would also invite Roger, Paule's official escort, and ten other people.

Roger accepted. He wanted to take a closer look at this young buck who followed Paule everywhere and of whom she spoke with an affection which was more reassuring to him than any restraint. Besides, he had a conscience about Paule, for he had neglected her over the past month. But he was infatuated with Maisy, with her stupidity, her body, with the appalling scenes she made, with her morbid jealousy, and not least with the unexpected passion which she harboured for him and daily threw in his face with a shamelessness that entranced him. He had the impression of living in a Turkish bath; he dimly reflected that this was the last passion-in-the-raw he would ever inspire; he surrendered to it, ringing Paule to cancel a date ('All right darling, tomorrow then,' she would say in her even voice) before returning to the frightful little boudoir where Maisy, with tears in her eyes, swore she would give up her career for him, if only he said the word. He observed himself with curiosity, wondering just how much stupidity he could stand; then he took her in his arms, she started cooing again and from the part-idiotic, part-obscene phrases she murmured he derived an erotic excitement such as he had rarely known. By providing Paule with company, therefore, young Van den Besh was in all innocence being very useful. As soon as he was through with Maisy, he would straighten things out; come to that, he would marry Paule. He was sure of nothing, nor of himself: the only thing he had ever been sure of was Paule's indestructible love and, these last few years, his own attachment to her.

He arrived a little late and realized at a glance that this was just the kind of dinner at which he would be bored to death. Paule often reproached him with his lack of sociability; and indeed, outside his work he saw no one, except for very specific purposes or else, as with Paule and a solitary friend, to talk. He lived alone; he could not stand certain social gatherings of a type all too frequent in Paris; he immediately wanted to behave crudely or walk out. This one was attended by a few select persons, well known in their sphere or by the newspapers and indubitably charming as well: over dinner the talk would be of plays or films or, worse still, of love and relationships between men and women, a topic which he particularly dreaded for he had the feeling of being quite unversed in it or, at the very least, incapable of formulating what knowledge he had. He greeted them all haughtily, holding his large frame a trifle stiffly and deriving, as always, the impression that his arrival had caused a draught – an impression which was not entirely unjustified, for he always created a diversion, so unassailable (and hence, to certain women, desirable) did he appear in the very first words of a conversation. Paule was wearing the dress he loved – a black one, cut lower than her others – and stooping towards her he gave her an acknowledging smile: she was the one acknowledgeable person in the room. And she shut her eyes for a moment, wishing desperately that he would take her in his arms. He sat down beside her. Only then did he spot the motionless figure of Simon. He thought how pained the boy must be by his presence and instinctively withdrew the arm he had slipped behind Paule's back. She turned, and abruptly, in the midst of the general hubbub, there was a three-cornered silence, intense between two of the parties and broken only by Simon's leaning forward to give Paule a light. Roger looked at them, at Simon's lanky figure, his earnest, rather too delicate profile inclined towards Paule's grave one, and a kind of irreverent laughter took hold of him. They were reserved, sensitive, well bred: he offered her a light, she refused him her body ('Thank you; no thank you'). The moment was rich in undertones. He, Roger, was made of different stuff: a little slut awaited him with the most commonplace pleasures, and, after her, the

Paris night and a thousand chance meetings; then, at dawn, came exhausting, almost manual work with men of his own kind, weary-limbed men doing jobs that he had once done. At that moment Paule said: 'Thank you' in her tranquil voice, and he could not prevent himself from taking her hand and squeezing it to call her back to him. He loved her. This little boy might drag her off to concerts and art galleries, but he would get nowhere. He rose, took a glass of Scotch from a tray, drained it at a gulp, and felt better.

The meal went along as he had anticipated. He emitted a few grunts, tried to say something and came to with a start to find Mrs Van den Besh asking him, with an obvious desire to supply the answer, if he knew who X slept with. He replied that he was no more interested in who X slept with than in what he ate, that the first item was no more important in his eyes than the second, and that society would do better to concern itself with people's tables than with their beds, thus occasioning them a good deal less trouble. Paule laughed, for by these words he had demolished the whole evening's talk, and Simon could not help following suit. Roger had drunk too much; he reeled a little as he stood up and failed to notice that Mrs Van den Besh was simperingly patting the chair beside her.

'My mother wants you,' said Simon.

They were face to face. Roger looked at him and searched hazily for a weak chin or mouth. The fact that he did not find them put him out of temper.

'And I suppose Paule is looking for you?'

'I'm going to her,' said Simon, and he turned on his heel.

Roger caught him by the elbow. He was suddenly furious. The young man stared at him in surprise.

'Wait . . . I have something to ask you.'

They surveyed one another, each of them conscious that there was nothing to be said, yet. But Roger was amazed at his action and Simon was so proud of it that he smiled. Roger understood; he released him.

'I wanted to ask you for a cigar.'

'But of course . . .'

Roger followed him with his eyes. Then he walked over to Paule, who was talking to a group of people, and took her by the arm. She trailed after him and at once fired a question.

'What did you say to Simon?'

'I asked him for a cigar. What were you afraid I'd said?'

'I don't know,' she said, relieved. 'You looked furious.'

'Why should I be furious? He's just a kid. Do you think I'm jealous?'

'No,' she said, and she lowered her gaze.

'If I *were* jealous, it would more likely be of your other neighbour at table. At least he's a man.'

For a moment she wondered whom he was referring to; when she realized, she could not help smiling. She had not even noticed him. For her, the whole meal had been illuminated by Simon, whose eyes, like beacons, had skimmed her face regularly every two minutes, a little blatant in their attempts to catch hers. Occasionally she had responded, and then he had treated her to such a tender, such an anxious, smile that she'd had to return it. He was infinitely more handsome, more alive than her other neighbour, and she reflected that Roger did not know what he was talking about. At all events, Simon came up to them and held a box of cigars out to Roger.

'Thank you,' said Roger. He selected one with care. 'You're too young to know what a good cigar is. That's a luxury reserved for men of my age.'

'You're welcome to it,' said Simon. 'I loathe the things.'

'Paule, you haven't taken a dislike to smoke? Anyway, we'll soon be going home,' he said, turning back to face Simon. 'I have to be up early.'

Simon was not impressed by the 'we'. He thought: that means he'll drop her outside her place and rush back to that little tart, leaving me here without her. He glanced at Paule, felt her read the same thought in her eyes, and murmured: 'If Paule isn't tired . . . I can drive her back later.'

They turned to her of one accord. She smiled at Simon and decided that she would rather go home: it was getting late.

In the car they did not say a word. Paule was waiting. Roger had dragged her away from a party she was enjoying; he owed her an explanation, or an excuse. He drew up opposite the flat and left the engine running ... and at once she realized that he had nothing to say, that he would not be coming up, that all this had been merely proprietary cautiousness on his part. She got out, murmured 'Good night', and crossed the road. Roger drove off at once; he was angry with himself.

But parked near the entrance was Simon's car, with Simon inside it. He hailed her and she went up to him in astonishment.

'How did you get here? You must have driven like mad. And what about your mother's party?'

'Get in for a moment,' he begged.

They whispered in the dark, as though someone might hear them. She slipped adroitly into the little car and realized it had become a habit – like the trusting face turned towards her and bisected by the light of the street-lamp.

'You weren't too bored?' he said.

'No, no ... I ...'

He was close beside her: too close, she thought. It was too late for talking, and he'd had no cause to follow her. Roger might have seen him, the whole thing was ridiculous ... she kissed Simon.

The winter wind was getting up in the streets; it blew across the open car, driving their hair between them; Simon was covering her face with kisses; in a daze she inhaled his young man's smell, his gasps, and the night chill. She left him without a word.

At dawn she half-woke and saw again, as in a dream, the dark mass of Simon's hair tangled with hers by the arctic wind, lingering between their faces like a silken screen; and she thought she could still feel his warm mouth burrowing into her. She went back to sleep smiling.

II

IT was ten days now since he had seen her. The morning after that crazy, tender evening when she had kissed him he had received a note from her, enjoining him not to try to see her again. 'I should only hurt you and I am too fond of you.' He had not realized that she was less afraid for him than for herself; he had believed in her pity and had not even been angry, merely searching for a means, a concept, which would enable him to envisage life without her. He did not pause to consider that these precautionary phrases — 'I should hurt you too much', 'It wouldn't be wise', and so forth — are often the quotation marks surrounding an affair, coming immediately before, or immediately after, but on no account discouraging. Paule did not know this, either. She had been afraid; she was unconsciously waiting for him to come for her and force her to accept his love. She was at the end of her tether. The monotony of the winter days; the endless procession of unchanging streets through which she made her solitary way from flat to shop; that treacherous telephone (Roger sounded so distant and ashamed that she was always sorry she had answered it); and finally a yearning for a long, never rediscovered summer — everything conspired to bring her to a state of defenceless passivity in which something *had* to happen.

Simon got down to work. He was punctual, conscientious, and withdrawn. From time to time, he looked up, stared vacantly at Madame Alice and drew a hesitant finger across his lips ... The abrupt, almost commanding way in which Paule, that last evening, had pressed her mouth to his, then thrown back her head and used both her hands to hold his face gently against hers. The wind ... Madame Alice cleared her throat, embarrassed by his stare, and he gave a faint smile. It had been a fit of spleen on Paule's part, that was all. He had not tried to follow her afterwards – had he perhaps been wrong? Ten or twenty times he went over the slightest incidents in the preceding weeks: their last drive together, that incredibly boring exhibition they had fled from, that infernal dinner at his mother's ... and every detail, every image, every possibility pained him a little more. Yet the days passed; he was gaining time, or wasting his life; he did not know where he was any more.

One evening he walked down a dark staircase with a friend and found himself in a small night club which he had never visited. They had drunk a lot; they ordered some more and grew sad again. Then a Negress came on to sing; she had a huge pink mouth; she opened up a thousand longings, she kindled the fires of a hopeless sentimentality to which they succumbed together.

'I'd give two years of my life to be in love with someone,' said Simon's friend.

'I *am* in love,' said Simon. 'And she'll never know I loved her. Never.'

He refused to enlarge on this, but at the same time it seemed to him that nothing was lost, that it was not possible: this flood of feeling within him to no purpose! They asked the singer over for a drink: she was from Pigalle, but she sang as though she were straight from New Orleans, filling Simon's reeling brain with a blue and tender life, full of proffered hands and faces. He stayed very late, listening to her all alone, and got home at dawn, quite sober.

*

At six next evening Simon stood waiting for Paule outside her shop. It was raining; he buried his hands in his pockets; he was angry to find them shaking. He felt strangely empty and limp. My God, he thought, perhaps I'm no good at anything with her now, except to feel pain. And he grimaced in disgust.

At half past six, Paule came out. She was wearing a dark suit and a blue-grey scarf that matched her eyes. She looked tired. He took a step towards her, she smiled at him, and in a flash he felt invaded by such a feeling of peace and plenty that he shut his eyes. He loved her. Whatever happened to him, so long as it was through her, he had nothing to lose. Paule saw his blindman's face, his outstretched hands, and she stopped. She had missed him, it was true, these last ten days. His continual presence, his admiration, his persistency had created, she thought, a kind of tangible habit which she had no reason to break. But the face he thrust towards her had nothing to do with habit, nor with the morale of a woman of thirty-nine. It was something quite different. The grubby pavement, the passers-by, the cars – everything round them suddenly struck her as a timeless, stylized, unchanging backcloth. They looked at each other from a distance of two yards, and before she could succumb again to the noisy, drab reality of the street, while she was still awake, alert, at the limits of her consciousness, Simon stepped forward and took her in his arms.

He held her loosely against him, unable to breathe yet possessed of a great calm. He laid his cheek on her hair and stared straight ahead of him at the sign over a bookshop: 'The Treasures of Time', dimly wondering how many treasures there could be in the shop, and how many throw-outs. At the same time, he was amazed that he should ask himself such an absurd question at just that moment. He had the impression of having finally solved a problem.

*

'Simon,' said Paule, 'how long have you been here? You must be wet through.'

She inhaled the smell of his tweed jacket, his neck, and had no desire to move. His return had brought her unexpected relief, almost a feeling of deliverance.

'You know,' said Simon, 'I simply couldn't live without you. I was all at sea. I wasn't even bored: I was cut off from myself. How about you?'

'Me?' said Paule. 'Oh, Paris isn't too bright at the moment.' She was trying to introduce a normal note to the conversation. 'I looked at a new collection, played the career woman, met a couple of Americans. There's talk of my going to New York . . .'

At the same time, she was thinking that it was useless taking this tone when they were standing in the rain, with their arms round each other, like two ecstatic lovers; but she could not move. Simon's mouth came lightly to rest on her temples, her hair, her cheek, punctuating her sentences. She broke off and nestled her head a little closer to his shoulder.

'Are you keen to go to New York?' said Simon's voice above her.

As he spoke, she felt his jawbone working against her head. It made her want to laugh like a schoolgirl.

'The States is sure to be fun, don't you think? I've never been.'

'Nor me,' said Simon. 'My mother couldn't stand it there; but then, she has always hated travel.'

He could have talked to her for hours about his mother, the urge to travel, America and Russia. He wanted to treat her to a hundred commonplaces, to make her a hundred unassuming, effortless speeches. He no longer thought of dazzling her or seducing her. He felt fine, at once frail and self-assured. He would have to take her home to kiss her properly, but he dared not let go of her.

'I need time to think,' said Paule.

And she herself did not know whether she was referring to him or her trip. She, too, was afraid:

afraid of looking up and seeing that youthful face next to hers, afraid of encountering the same old Paule, strong-willed and moderate. Afraid of judging herself.

'Simon,' she murmured.

He stooped and kissed her lightly on the lips. They kept their eyes open and all each could see of the other was a huge twinkling blur, full of gleams and shadows: an immeasurably enlarged pupil, liquid, terrified almost.

Two days later they dined together. Paule had only to say a few words for Simon to realize what those ten days had been like for her: Roger's jibes and indifference, her loneliness. No doubt Paule had hoped to turn the interval to account in winning Roger back, or at least in seeing him and restoring their old relationship. But she had been up against an impatient child. Her efforts, so touching in their modesty – dinner served just as he liked it, plus his favourite dress, plus a conversation on his pet topic – all those devices which, in women's magazines, seem so many paltry baits, but which, in the hands of an intelligent woman, are terribly affecting, had been to no avail. And she had not felt humiliated at using them; she had not even been ashamed to substitute skilful lighting or a tender leg of lamb for the phrases burning on her lips: 'Roger, you're making me miserable', 'Roger, this can't go on.' When she came to think about it, she had behaved in this way not from any inherited instinct as a housewife, nor even from bitter acceptance. No, she had acted, rather, from a kind of sadism towards 'them', towards what they had been together. As though one of them, he or she, should have leaped up and said: 'That's enough.' And she had awaited this reaction from herself almost as anxiously as from Roger. But in vain. Perhaps something had died.

So, after ten days of wasted schemes and misplaced hopes, she could only be conquered by Simon. Simon saying: 'I'm so happy, I love you,' without the words sounding insipid; Simon stammering on the telephone; Simon bringing her something whole, or at least the whole half of something. She knew well enough that two were needed for this kind of thing; but she had grown tired, these last years, of always being the first and apparently the only one. 'To love is nothing,' Simon told her, speaking of himself, 'one must also be loved.' And this had struck her as strangely personal. Only, on the threshold of this new affair, she was astonished to feel – in place of the excitement, the glow which had ushered in her relationship with Roger, for instance – only a vast, tender weariness which affected even the way she walked. Everyone advised a change of air, and she thought sadly that all she was getting was a change of lovers: less bother, more Parisian, so common . . . And she shied away from her own face in the mirror, or covered it with cold cream. But when Simon rang the door-bell that evening and she saw his dark tie, his anxious eyes, the intense joy of his whole appearance, and his embarrassment too (like someone spoiled by life and striking lucky yet again), she wanted to share his happiness. The happiness she gave him: 'Here is my body, my warmth, and my tenderness; they are no good to me, but perhaps in your hands, they will acquire a certain new savour for me.' He spent the night in her arms.

She imagined the tone in which people – her friends – would say: 'Have you heard about Paule?' And more than fear of gossip, more than fear at the difference in their ages (which, as she very well knew, would be carefully emphasized), it was shame that gripped her. Shame at the thought of the gaiety with which people would spread the story, of the pep with which they would credit her, the appetite for life and young men, whereas she merely felt old and tired and in need of a little comforting. And it sickened her to think they were now in a position to treat her at once savagely and fawningly, as she had seen them treat others a hundred times over. They had called her 'Poor Paule', because Roger was deceiving her, or spoken of her 'mad independence'; when she had left a young, good-looking, boring husband they had condemned or pitied her. But they had never shown her the mixture of contempt and envy she was going to arouse this time.

12

CONTRARY to Paule's belief, Simon did not sleep during their first night together. He restricted himself to holding her to him, his hand resting on a slight fold at her waist; he lay quite still, listening to her regular breathing and adapting his own to it. You have to be very much in love or very disgusted to feign sleep, he thought hazily; and he, who was accustomed only to the second condition, watched over Paule's sleep as zealously as the vestals guarding their sacred fire. Thus they spent their night side by side, each protecting the other's counterfeit sleep, fondly and thoughtfully, not daring to move.

Simon was happy. He felt more responsible for Paule, though she was fourteen years his senior, than for a sixteen-year-old virgin. While still marvelling at Paule's acquiescence and, for the first time, feeling that what had happened had been in the nature of a gift, he thought it indispensable that he should watch over her intently, as though to protect her in advance from the harm he might one day do her. He kept watch, he mounted guard against his own dastardliness, his clowning, his terrors, his sudden fits of boredom, his weakness. He would make her happy, he would be happy himself, and he told himself with amazement that he had never sworn such oaths even in the course of his greatest conquests.

Thus when morning came there were several false awakenings, first one, then the other – but never the two together – going through the motions of a yawn, a contented stretching of limbs. When Simon turned over or propped himself up on one elbow, Paule would instinctively bury herself under the sheets, afraid of what his expression might be – that first expression after the act of love, more commonplace and decisive than any gesture. And when, her patience now exhausted, she in turn started moving about, Simon – equally on his guard, though his eyes were closed, and already afraid of losing the happiness he had found in the night – held his breath. Finally she caught him looking at her from under his lids by the pallid daylight filtering through the curtains, and she froze, facing him. She felt old and ugly; she stared fixedly at him so that he should see her clearly, so that at least there should be no early morning uncertainties between them. Simon, his eyes still not properly open, smiled, murmured her name, and slid beside her. 'Simon,' she said, and she stiffened, still trying to pass the night off as a caprice. He laid his head on her heart and gently kissed her, at the bend of the arm, on the shoulder, on the cheek, hugging her to him. 'I dreamed of you,' he said. 'I shall never dream of anyone but you.' She closed her arms about him.

Simon wanted to drive her to work, stipulating that he would drop her at the corner if she preferred. She replied, rather sadly, that she was not answerable to anyone, and there was a momentary silence between them. It was Simon who broke it.

'Won't you be free before six? Can you have lunch with me?'

'I haven't time,' she said. 'I shall have a sandwich in the shop.'

'What am I going to do until six?' he groaned.

She looked at him. She was perturbed: could she tell him that there was no law which said they had to meet at six? On the other hand, the thought of his being there, outside the shop, impatient in his little car every evening, brought her real happiness ... Someone who waited for you every evening, someone who did not ring you up vaguely, at eight or after, when he felt like it ... She smiled.

'How do you know I haven't a dinner engagement this evening?'

Simon, who was having difficulty with his cufflinks, stopped wrestling with them. After a moment he said: 'True, I don't,' in a neutral voice. He was thinking of Roger, of course! He thought only of Roger; he visualized him ready to reclaim his property; he was afraid. But she knew Roger was not thinking of her. The whole thing struck her as hateful. Let her at least be generous!

'I've no engagement this evening,' she said. 'Come here and let me help you with those.'

She was sitting on the bed and he knelt in front of her, holding out his arms as if his sleeves had been fetters. He had a boy's wrists, smooth and slender. As she fastened the links, Paule suddenly had the feeling of having played this scene before. That's very theatrical, she thought, but she laid her cheek on Simon's hair with a small, happy laugh.

'And what am I going to do until six?' he persisted.

'I don't know . . . you're going to work.'

'I shan't be able to,' he said. 'I'm too happy.'

'That doesn't stop people from working!'

'Me it does. Besides, I know what I'll do. I'll drive around and think of you, then I'll lunch alone, thinking of you, and then I'll wait for six o'clock. I'm not one of your energetic types.'

'What will your lawyer friend say?'

'I don't know. Why should I waste my time preparing for my future when only my present interests me. And overwhelms me,' he added with a sweeping bow.

Paule shrugged. But Simon did exactly as he had said, that day and the days that followed. He motored about Paris, smiling at everyone; ten times he drove past Paule's shop, at ten miles an hour; he read a book, parking anywhere, laying it down at times to throw back his head and shut his eyes. He had the look of a happy sleepwalker, and this did not fail to move Paule and endear him to her more. She had the impression of giving and was amazed that this should suddenly strike her as almost indispensable.

*

Roger had been travelling for ten days, in appalling weather, rushing from one business dinner to another, and the northern province was symbolized for him by an interminable slippery road and the characterless interiors of restaurants. From time to time he put through a call to Paris, asking for two numbers at the same time, and listened to the complaints of Maisy-Marcelle before complaining to Paule – or after. He felt despondent, helpless, his life resembled this province. Paule's voice was changing, becoming at once more anguished and more distant; he wanted to see her again. He had never been able to spend a fortnight away from her without missing her. In Paris, of course, where he knew she was always ready to see him, always at his disposal, he could space out their meetings; but Lille restored her to him as she had been right at the beginning, when his life had depended entirely on hers and he had been as afraid of conquering her as he was now afraid of losing her. On the last day of his travels, he announced his return. There was a silence, then at once she resumed: 'I've got to see you.' The words had a final ring. He asked no questions, but arranged to meet her next day.

He returned to Paris that night and at two in the morning was outside Paule's. For the first time, he hesitated to go up. He was not sure of finding that same happy face, forcing itself to be calm, which his surprises usually prompted; he was afraid. He waited ten minutes, self-impeded, providing himself with poor excuses – 'She'll be asleep, she works too hard,' and so forth – then drove off. Outside his own flat, he hesitated again, then suddenly swung the car round and drove to Maisy's. She was asleep; waking, she thrust a puffy face towards him. She had been out very late, she said, with her inevitable producers . . . she was so happy . . . as a matter of fact, she had just been dreaming about him, etc. He undressed rapidly and went straight off to sleep, despite her provocations. For the first time, he did not want her. At dawn he complied mechanically, laughed a little at her gossip, and decided that everything was all right. He spent the morning in her flat and left her ten minutes before his rendezvous with Paule.

13

'I must make a phone call,' said Paule. 'After lunch will be too late.'

Roger stood up as she left the table, and Paule gave him that brief, apologetic smile which she could not deny herself whenever she obliged him, through the conventions of society or of the heart, to put himself out for her. She thought of this with irritation as she walked down the dank stairway which led to the telephone. With Simon, it was different. He was so keen, so glad, so prompt to look after her, to open doors for her, to light her cigarettes, to anticipate her slightest wishes, that he had come to think of these things before she did, making them seem a series of attentions rather than obligations. That morning she had left him half-asleep, his arms round his pillow, his dark locks tousled, and she had written him a note: 'Will ring at twelve.' But at twelve she had met Roger and now she was amazed to find herself leaving him alone at table so as to telephone a lazy young lover. Would he notice? His brow was furrowed and anxious, as it always was on his off-days; he seemed older.

Simon picked up the receiver at once. He laughed the moment she said hullo, and she laughed too.

'You're awake, then?'

'I've been awake since eleven. It's one now. I've

already rung the operator to find out whether the telephone was out of order.'

'Why?'

'You were supposed to call me at twelve. Where are you?'

'At Luigi's. I'm about to have lunch.'

'I see,' said Simon.

There was a silence. In the end she added baldly: 'I'm lunching with Roger.'

'I see.'

'Is that all you can say?' she said. ' "I see . . ." I shall be back at the shop by two-thirty at the latest. What are you doing?'

'I'm going round to my mother's for some clothes,' said Simon very quickly. 'I'm coming back here to hang them up and then I'm going to get that water-colour that caught your eye in Desnos's.'

For a moment she wanted to laugh. It was typical of Simon to run two sentences together like that.

'Why? Are you thinking of using my place as a changing-room?'

At the same time she cast around for serious arguments to dissuade him. But what were they? He hardly ever left her, and she had not reproached him up to now . . .

'Yes,' said Simon. 'There are too many people hanging round you. I mean to be your watchdog, and for that I need clean clothes.'

'We'll talk about it later,' she said.

She had the impression she had been on the phone for an hour. Roger was upstairs alone. He was sure to ask questions, and she could not rid herself of a feeling of guilt.

'I love you,' said Simon, before he hung up.

On her way out, she automatically gave her hair a quick comb in the cloakroom mirror. She was staring at a face to which someone said: 'I love you.'

Roger was drinking a cocktail and Paule was surprised, knowing that he never touched alcohol during the day.

'Is something wrong?'

'Why? Oh, the gin! No, I'm just tired.'

'It's a long time since I've seen you,' she said, and, as he rather absent-mindedly agreed, she felt the tears prick at her eyes. The day would come when they would say: 'Is it two months since we met, or three?' And they would quietly tot it up. Roger, with his quaint gestures and his tired face, that childish look in spite of his strength, his near-cruelty . . . She averted her head. He was wearing his old grey jacket which she had seen, almost new, draped on a chair in her bedroom, at the start of their affair. He was very proud of it. He seldom gave much thought to being elegant, and anyway he was rather on the heavy side ever really to be so.

'A fortnight,' she said calmly. 'Are you well?'

'Yes. Not bad, anyway.'

He broke off. No doubt he was waiting for her to say: 'And how's work?', but she didn't. First she was going to have to tell him about Simon; then he would be able to confide in her without later having the feeling that he had made a fool of himself.

'Have you been enjoying yourself?' he said.

She froze. A pulse raced in her temples; she felt her heart wither. She heard herself say: 'Yes, I've been seeing Simon. A lot.'

'Ah!' said Roger. 'That charming boy? Still stuck on you?'

She nodded her head slowly and once too often, without looking up.

'You still find him fun?' said Roger.

She raised her eyes, but it was his turn not to look at her: he was concentrating hard on his grapefruit. She thought: he has realized.

'Yes,' she said.

'You find him fun? Or more than that?'

They were looking at each other now all right. Roger laid down his spoon. With demented fondness she registered the two long lines beside his mouth, the impassive face, the faintly ringed blue eyes.

'More than that,' she said.

Roger's hand strayed back to the spoon and closed on it. He has never known the proper way to eat a grapefruit, she thought. Time seemed at once to be standing still and whistling in her ears.

'I suppose there's nothing I can say,' said Roger.

And at this she knew he was unhappy. Had he been happy, he would have remonstrated with her. But he sat there as though her admission were the last straw.

She murmured: 'There was everything you could have said.'

'You yourself put it in the past.'

'To spare you, Roger. If I told you that everything still depends on you, what could you say?'

He said nothing. He stared at the table-cloth.

She continued: 'You would tell me you are too taken up with your freedom, too frightened of losing it to . . . well, to make the necessary effort to get me back.'

'I tell you I just don't know,' snapped Roger. 'Obviously I loathe the idea of your . . . Is he gifted, at least?'

'It isn't a question of gifts of that sort,' she said. 'He loves me.'

She saw him relax slightly and for a moment she detested him. He was reassured: this was just an emotional fit on her part; he was still her real lover, the he-man.

'Though obviously,' she added, 'I can't say he leaves me cold in certain matters.'

That's the first time, she thought bewilderedly, that I have ever deliberately hurt him.

'I must confess,' said Roger, 'that when I asked you out to lunch, I didn't expect to be treated to an account of your antics with a schoolboy.'

'You expected me to imagine yours with a schoolgirl,' returned Paule.

'That's more normal, anyway,' he said through his teeth.

Paule was shaking. She picked up her handbag and got to her feet.

'I suppose you're going to throw my age in my face?'

97

'Paule . . .'

Rising in turn, he followed her through the swing-doors. She stumbled, blind with tears. He caught up with her at her car. She was tugging fruitlessly at the starter. He reached through the window and turned on the ignition, which she had forgotten. Roger's hand . . . She turned a distraught face towards him.

'Paule . . . you know very well . . . That was vile of me. Forgive me. You know I wasn't thinking that.'

'I know,' she said. 'I was spiteful too. It would be better if we didn't see each other for a time.'

He stood there, looking lost. She gave him a brief smile.

'*Au revoir, mon chéri.*'

He stooped towards the window.

'I think the world of you, Paule.'

She drove off very fast so that he should not see the tears that blurred her vision. Mechanically she turned on the windscreen-wipers, and her action wrenched a small, broken laugh from her. It was half past one. She had plenty of time to go home, recover and fix her make-up. She at once hoped and dreaded that Simon had gone. She ran into him in the entrance hall.

'Paule . . . what's the matter?'

She did not answer. In the lift, he wrapped his arms round her, drank her tears, begged her not to cry any more, and swore indistinctly to 'kill the swine' (at which she had to smile).

'I must be a terrible woman,' she said, and she had the impression that she had read the line a thousand times, or heard it in a hundred films.

Later, she sank on to the divan beside Simon and took his hand.

'Don't ask me anything,' she said.

'Not today. But one day I shall ask you everything. Very soon. I can't bear people making you cry. And most of all, I can't bear him succeeding,' he shouted angrily. 'What about me? Shall I never be able to make you cry . . . ?'

She looked at him: men really were savages.

'Are you so keen to?'

'I would rather be in pain myself,' said Simon, and he buried his face in Paule's neck.

When she got back in the evening, he had drunk three-quarters of a bottle of Scotch and had not even been out. He declared with great dignity that he'd had personal worries, launched into a speech on the difficulty of existence, and fell asleep on the bed while she was taking off his shoes. She was half moved, half alarmed.

*

Roger was standing at the window, watching the dawn. It was one of those residential farms in the Île-de-France where the countryside came strangely close to the mental picture formed by the town-sick. With quiet hills, rich fields, and hoardings all along the roads. But then, at that strange hour of daybreak, it was the real, remote countryside of childhood which came to haunt Roger with the oppressive, chilly smell of rain. He turned and said: 'Damned fine weather for a week-end,' but he was thinking: 'It's wonderful. I love this mist. If only I could be alone.' In the warmth of her bed, Maisy turned over.

'Shut the window,' she said. 'It's cold.'

She pulled the sheet over her shoulder. Despite the languid contentment of her body, she was already appalled by the thought of the day ahead, in this isolated spot, with Roger sullen and distant and those fields stretching away for as far as the eye could see . . . She wanted to groan.

'I asked you to shut the window,' she said tartly.

He had lit a Gauloise, the first of the day, and was savouring its almost unpleasant yet somehow delightful bitterness, already plucked from his morning daydreams and feeling, with a kind of impatience, Maisy's hostility mounting at his back. Let her get mad, he thought! Let her jump out of bed and take the coach back to Paris! I shall spend the whole day walking through the fields; I'm sure to find a stray dog to keep me company (he had a horror of being alone).

Yet after her second injunction Maisy hesitated. She could forget about the window and go back to sleep, or she could make a scene. In her befogged brain there fluttered such lines as: 'I am a woman who is cold. He is a man who ought to shut the window.' At the same time her intuition, awake bright and early that morning, warned her against provoking Roger.

She took a moderate line.

'You should shut the window and order breakfast, *chéri*.'

Roger swung round in disappointment and said at random: ' "*Chéri*"? What does "*chéri*" mean?'

She laughed. He went on: 'I didn't ask you to laugh, I merely asked you what "*chéri*" means. Do you cherish me? Do you know the verb "to cherish" other than by hearsay?'

I really must have had enough of her, he thought, amazed at his own words; when I start worrying about a woman's vocabulary, the end is in sight.

'What's got into you?' said Maisy.

From the bedclothes emerged her face (horror-stricken, almost), which he found comic, and her breasts, which he no longer desired. Indecent! She was indecent!

'Feelings are very important,' he said. 'For you, I'm just a passing fancy. A convenient one. So don't call me "*chéri*", especially in the morning; at night, okay!'

'But Roger,' protested Maisy, understandably alarmed, 'I love you.'

'Oh no! Don't say anything! – anything at all!' he shouted, with a mixture of embarrassment, for at heart he wasn't a bad fellow, and relief, for his remark reduced their situation to the classic and, to him, familiar one of a man sick to death of an inopportune affair.

He pulled his sweater down over his trousers and went out. He wished he were wearing his jacket, but fetching it would have meant walking right round the bed, and the manoeuvre would have impaired the speed essential for his exit. Outside, he inhaled the icy air and a kind of dizziness took hold of him. He had to return to Paris, and there was no Paule waiting for him. The car would skid on the wet roads, he would have coffee at the Porte d'Auteuil in dead, Sunday-morning Paris. He went back inside to pay his bill, then drove off like a burglar. Maisy would bring his jacket with her; he would send his secretary round to her flat for it, with some flowers. For I don't know how to do things, he thought without gaiety.

For a time he drove in silence, frowning to himself; then he reached for the radio and remembered. Cherish, he thought, cherish – that was Paule and me. Life had no flavour for him. He had lost her.

14

A WEEK later, in the flat, the smell of tobacco caught at Paule's throat. She opened the sitting-room window, called 'Simon!' and received no answer. For a moment she was afraid, and this amazed her. She walked over to the bedroom door and opened it. Simon lay there asleep, his shirt open at the neck. She called him a second time and he did not stir. She returned to the living-room, opened a cupboard, looked at the whisky bottle, and replaced it with a brief grimace of distaste. She looked about her for a glass, failed to find one, and went out to the kitchen. There was a wet glass on the draining-board. She stood stock-still for a second or two, then slowly took off her coat. In the bathroom, she carefully made herself up and tidied her hair. She laid the brush down hurriedly, chiding herself for her coquetry as though it were a weakness. Much point there was in trying to please Simon!

Back in the bedroom, she shook him and switched on the bedside lamp. He stretched, murmured her name, and turned back to face the wall.

'Simon,' she said curtly.

His movement had uncovered Paule's scarf – he must have buried his face in it before falling asleep. She had chaffed him about his fetishism often enough. But she was in no mood to laugh. She felt in the grips of a cold anger. She turned him towards the light. He opened his eyes, smiled, and at once stopped smiling.

'What's up?'

'I've got to talk to you.'

'I knew it,' he said, and he sat up on the bed.

She rose, for she'd had to restrain an impulse to brush away the strand of black hair which hung over his eyes. She leaned against the window.

'Simon, this can't go on. This is the last time I shall tell you. You must work. It's come to the point where you drink on the sly.'

'I've just rinsed the glass. You hate untidiness.'

'I hate untidiness, lies, and weakness,' she burst out. 'I'm beginning to hate you.'

He was off the bed. She could feel him standing behind her, looking crestfallen. She deliberately refrained from turning.

'I knew you couldn't stand me any more,' he said. 'It's a short step from quite liking someone to not liking him at all . . .'

'It isn't a question of feelings, Simon. It's a question of your drinking, of your doing nothing, of your besotting yourself. I've told you to work. I've told you a hundred times. This is the last.'

'And then what?'

'I shan't be able to see you any more,' she said.

'You could leave me just like that,' he said thoughtfully.

'Yes.'

She turned to him and opened her mouth to speak.

'Listen, Simon . . .'

He was sitting on the bed again, staring at his hands with an odd expression. He slowly raised them and put them to his face. She was thunderstruck. He did not cry, he did not move, and it seemed to Paule that she had never seen anyone in such utter despair. She murmured his name, as though to pluck him from some danger the nature of which she could not conceive, then went up to him. He was gently rocking himself on the edge of the bed, still keeping his face hidden. She thought for a moment he was drunk, and reached out to stop his swaying. Then she tried to remove his hands; he resisted, and in the end she knelt facing him and took hold of his wrists.

'Simon, look at me . . . Simon, stop play-acting.'

She drew his hands away and he looked at her. He had the smooth, perfectly impassive face of certain statues, and the same blind stare. Instinctively she put her own hand over his eyes.

'What's wrong? Simon . . . Tell me what's wrong . . .'

He bent a little further forward, laid his head on her shoulder with a sigh, like someone very tired.

'You don't love me, that's what,' said Simon evenly, 'and there's nothing I can do about it. And I knew right from the start you would throw me out. And I waited, bowing to the inevitable, yet hoping at times . . . That's the worst part, hoping at times, especially at night,' he said more softly, and she felt herself blush. 'And now today it's happened, and for a week I've felt it coming, and all the whisky in the world couldn't reassure me. And

I could feel you quietly hating me. That's what is wrong.' Then: 'Paule', he said, 'Paule . . .'

She folded her arms about him and hugged him to her, her eyes full of tears. She heard herself soothing him; 'Simon, you're crazy . . . you're only a child . . . My darling, my poor love . . .' She kissed him on the forehead and on the cheeks, and for a second she thought, with cruelty to herself, that she had finally reached the maternal stage. At the same time, something inside her persisted, delighted in cradling in Simon some old shared grief.

'You're tired,' she said. 'You've been so busy acting the abandoned lover that you've fooled even yourself. You mean a lot to me, Simon, more than I can say. My mind has been on my work lately, that's all.'

'Really all? You don't want me to leave?'

'Not today,' she said with a smile. 'But I do want you to work.'

'I'll do whatever you want,' he said. 'Lie down beside me, Paule. I've been so afraid! I need you. Kiss me. Keep still. I loathe these complicated dresses . . . Paule . . .'

Afterwards, she lay quite still. He was breathing gently beside her, exhausted, and laying her hand on the back of his neck she was invaded by a feeling of possession so painful and heart-rending that she thought she loved him.

Next day he went to work, smoothed things over with his chief, turned up a few files, rang Paule half a dozen times, borrowed some money from his mother (she was relieved to hear from him), and returned to Paule's at half past eight, looking weighed down with work. At the end of the day, he had killed two hours playing '421' in a bar, merely to engineer this triumphal return. Privately he reflected that his really was a very boring profession and that he was going to have a hard time filling in the idle spells.

15

NORMALLY Roger and Paule went away together in February for a week in the mountains. It had been agreed between them that, whatever their emotional involvements (only Roger's had then been in question), they should set aside a few peaceful days each winter. One morning Roger rang Paule at her office to say he was leaving in ten days' time and should he get a ticket for her? There was a silence. For a moment she wondered in terror what lay behind this invitation: instinctive need of her, remorse, or the desire to separate her from Simon? She might possibly have yielded to the first of these reasons. But she was well aware that, whatever he said to her, she would never be sure enough of him not to suffer a great deal during the holiday. At the same time, the memory of Roger in the mountains, brimming over with vitality, tearing down the slopes like a bullet and dragging her after him in terror, wrenched at her heart.

'Well?'

'I don't think it's possible, Roger. We should be making a pretence of . . . well, of not thinking of other things.'

'But that's the very reason why I'm going: to think of nothing. And I assure you I'm quite capable of it.'

'I'd come with you if you . . .' (she was going to

say: 'if you were capable of thinking of me, of us', but she checked herself) '. . . if you really needed me. But you'll get along fine by yourself or with . . . someone else.'

'Check. If I understand rightly, you don't want to leave Paris at the moment ?'

He's thinking of Simon, she said to herself: why can people never distinguish between appearance and reality ? At the same time she told herself that, for the past month, Simon's appearance had become her daily life. And perhaps she owed him the refusal which something had prompted her to make to Roger's proposal.

'If you like to put it that way,' she said.

There was a silence.

'You don't seem too fit at the moment, Paule. You looked tired when I saw you. If you don't like my arrangements, make others. You need to get away.'

His voice was warm and sad, and Paule felt the tears come into her eyes. Yes, she needed him; she needed him to protect her completely instead of suggesting these ten days on the cheap. He should have known that; there were limits to everything, even male egoism.

'Oh, I shall,' she said. 'We'll send each other postcards, peak to peak.'

He hung up. After all, he may merely have been asking for support, and she had refused it. A fine love hers was! But at the same time she felt confusedly that it was her prerogative, almost her duty, to be exacting and suffer for it. After all, there was someone who loved her passionately.

Up to now, she and Simon had always eaten alone in small local restaurants. But when she got home that evening she found him on the doorstep, looking very sedate in a dark suit, every hair in place. Once again she noticed his beauty, the feline length of his eyes, the perfect shape of his mouth, and she reflected with amusement that this little boy, who spent his days waiting for her buried under her dresses, had the looks of a Reiter and lady-killer.

'Such elegance!' she said. 'What goes on?'

'We're having an evening out,' he said. 'We're going to eat somewhere lavish and dance. I should be just as happy with a couple of fried eggs here, but I feel like taking you out.'

He helped her off with her coat. She noticed that he had smothered himself with toilet water. On the bed in her room lay a very low-cut cocktail dress which she had worn twice in her life.

'That's my favourite,' said Simon. 'Would you like a drink?'

He had mixed the kind she liked. Paule sat down on the bed, completely in a whirl: she had come down from the mountains to find herself faced with an evening out. She smiled at him.

'Are you pleased? You aren't tired, are you? If you like, I'll climb straight out of this suit and we'll stay here.'

He set one knee on the bed and went through the motions of taking off his jacket. She leaned against him, slid her hand under his shirt, felt the warmth of his skin against her palm. He was alive, so alive.

'It's a wonderful idea,' she said. 'Do you insist on this dress? I look a bit silly in it.'

'I love you naked,' he said, 'and this is the most naked you have. I had a good look.'

She reached for her cocktail and drank it. She might have come home to a lonely flat and gone rather gloomily to bed with a book, as she often had before he came along. But he was there, he was laughing, he was happy, she laughed with him and he was insistent she should teach him the Charleston, thus blithely putting twenty years on her, and she tripped on the carpet as she was dancing and fell breathless into his arms, and he hugged her to him, and she laughed more than ever, completely forgetting Roger and the snow and her sorrows. She was young, she was beautiful; she turned him out, made herself up to look rather like a vamp, and put on that indecent dress, and he pounded on the door in his impatience. When she emerged he looked at her in dazzlement and covered her shoulders with kisses. He made her have a second cocktail – with *her* head for drink! She was happy. Marvellously happy.

In the restaurant, at a table close to theirs, she recognized two women rather older than herself who occasionally worked with her and who now gave her a surprised smile. When Simon rose to escort her on to the floor she caught the phrase: '*How* old is she now?'

She leaned against Simon. Everything was spoiled. Her dress was ridiculous for her age, Simon rather too striking, and her life rather too absurd.

She asked Simon to take her home. He did not protest and she knew that he had heard, too.

She undressed very quickly. Simon was talking about the band. She would have liked to send him away. She stretched out in the dark while he undressed. She had been wrong to drink those two cocktails and the champagne; she would look haggard next day. She was almost dazed with gloom. Simon came back into the bedroom, sat down on the edge of the bed, and laid a hand on her forehead.

'Not tonight, Simon,' she said. 'I'm tired.'

He made no reply, but sat quite still. She could see his figure outlined against the light from the bathroom; his head was lowered and he seemed to be reflecting.

'Paule,' he said at last, 'I must talk to you.'

'It's late. I'm tired. Tomorrow.'

'No,' he said. 'I want to talk to you right away. And you're going to listen to me.'

She opened her eyes in amazement. This was the first time he had spoken to her in a tone of authority.

'I heard what those old hags behind us said. I won't have you upsetting yourself over it. It's unworthy of you, it's cowardly, and it's hurtful to me.'

'But Simon, you're making a tragedy out of nothing . . .'

'I'm not making a tragedy of it: on the contrary, I want to stop *you* from making tragedies out of such trifles. Naturally you would hide them from me. But you've no need to. I'm not a little boy, Paule. I'm quite capable of understanding you, and maybe of helping you. I'm very happy with you,

you know that, but my ambitions don't rest there: I want you to be happy with me. At present you're too bound up with Roger for that to happen. But you have got to start thinking of our affair as something positive, something on which you must help me to build, and not as a momentary windfall. There's what I had to say.'

He spoke calmly but with effort. Paule listened to him with astonishment and a kind of hope. She had thought him unaware; he wasn't, and he thought she could start all over again. Perhaps, after all, she could . . .?

'I'm not a fool, you know. I'm twenty-five, I hadn't lived before you came and I certainly shan't live after you've gone. You are the woman – more than that: the human being – I must have. I know it. If you liked, I'd marry you tomorrow.'

'I'm thirty-nine,' she said.

'Life isn't a woman's magazine, nor a cluster of reminiscences. You are fourteen years older than me, and I love you, and I shall love you for a very long time. That's all there is to it. So I won't have you sinking to the level of those old witches or of public opinion. The problem for you, for us, is Roger. There are no others.'

'Simon,' she said, 'I want you to forgive me for . . .well, for supposing . . .'

'You didn't believe I was capable of thinking, that's all. Now move over a bit.'

He slipped into bed beside her, kissed her, and took her. She did not complain of her tiredness, and he roused her to a pitch of pleasure such as she had not previously known with him. Afterwards he stroked her sweating brow, installed it in the hollow of his shoulder, reversing his usual practice, and carefully drew the bedclothes over her.

'Go to sleep,' he said. 'I'll take care of everything.'

In the darkness she gave a tender little smile and pressed her lips to his shoulder, a caress which he received with the olympian calm of a master. He lay awake for a long time, alarmed and impressed by his own firmness.

16

EASTER was approaching and Simon spent his days poring over maps hidden among his chief's files or strewn over Paule's carpet. To date he had planned two crowded itineraries for Italy and three for Spain, and was at present wavering towards Greece. Paule listened to him without saying anything: she would have ten days at most and she was feeling too tired even to catch a train. She would have liked a house in the country, a succession of identical days: childhood, in short! But she hadn't the heart to discourage Simon. Already he saw himself as the perfect traveller, leaping from the carriage to help her down on to the platform, guiding her to a car hired a fortnight beforehand, which would drive them to the best hotel in town, where their room would be full of the flowers he had telegraphed; he was forgetting that he had never yet managed to time a connexion or hold on to a ticket. He was dreaming, still dreaming, but all his dreams were directed at Paule, rushed headlong towards her like churning rivers towards a calm sea. He had never felt so free as in these last few months, when each day had found him at the same office, each evening with the same companion, in the same flat, clinging to the same desire, the same anxiety, the same pain. For Paule still broke away at times, avoided his eyes, smiled fondly at his impassioned speeches. Paule still said nothing when there was talk of Roger. Often he had the impression of waging an absurd, exhausting, and hopeless struggle, for, as he fully sensed, the passage of time was getting him nowhere. He had not simply to efface Paule's memory of Roger; he had to kill something inside her which *was* Roger, a kind of painful, ineradicable root which she endured with forbearance, and there were times when he reached the point of wondering whether it were not this forbearance, this accepted suffering that had first made him fall for her and now, perhaps, even kept his love alive. But generally he said to himself: 'Paule is waiting for me; in an hour I shall have her in my arms,' and it seemed to him that Roger had never existed, that Paule loved him, Simon, and that everything was simple and ablaze with happiness. And these were the times Paule preferred him – when he treated their relationship as an inescapable fact to which she could only subscribe. She was tired of her own diffidence. But when she was alone, the thought of Roger living without her would seem a fundamental mistake; she would ask herself how they had landed where they were. And 'they', 'we' still meant her and Roger. Simon was 'he'. Only, Roger knew nothing of this. When he was weary of his present life, he would come and grumble to her and no doubt try to win her back. And perhaps he would succeed. Simon would be well and truly hurt and she would be alone again, waiting for unreliable telephone calls and unfailing slights. And she rebelled against her own fatalism, against the impression that all this was inescapable. There was someone inescapable in her life: Roger.

But this did not prevent her from living with Simon, from sighing in his arms at night and sometime from holding him to her in response to one of those impulses which only children and slick lovers can inspire, an impulse so possessive, so terrified at the idea of the precariousness of all possession, that he himself did not notice its intensity. At these moments Paule was close to old age, to that incomparable love that comes with age, and afterwards she was angry with herself and angry with Roger (who did not compel her to withdraw into herself) for not being there. When Roger took her, he was her master, she was his property, he was only a year or two older than she, and everything complied with certain moral or aesthetic rules which she had never till then suspected herself of harbouring. But Simon did not feel himself to be her master. He had adopted, through an unconscious 'hamming' which he could not have supposed would lead to his downfall, a complete attitude of dependence which made him fall asleep on her shoulder, as though for protection, get up at dawn to make breakfast, and consult her over the smallest thing – an attitude which moved Paule, yet somehow embarrassed her, discomforted her, as though she were faced with something abnormal. She respected him: he was working now; on one occasion he had taken her to a trial, in Versailles, where he had given a remarkable performance as the young lawyer, shaking hands, smiling condescendingly at the journalists, and always returning to her as to the pivot of all his activity, at times interrupting his effusions to strangers so as to confirm that she was looking at him. No, he made no show of detachment. So she kept her eyes on him, putting every ounce of admiration and interest into her expression, which changed, the moment he turned his back, into one of affection and a certain pride. The women looked at him a good deal. She felt good: someone was living wholly for her. For her, at last, the question of the difference in their ages did not arise; she did not ask herself: 'And in ten years' time will he still love me?' In ten years' time, she would be alone or with Roger. Something inside her persisted in telling her this. And at the thought of this duplicity, which she could do nothing about, her fondness for Simon redoubled: 'My victim, my dear victim, my little Simon!' For the first time she was tasting the awful pleasure of loving somebody whom one is unavoidably going to hurt.

This 'unavoidably' and its consequences – the questions which Simon would one day ask her, which he would be entitled to ask her as a man she had hurt – appalled her. 'Why do you prefer Roger to me? What has that heel to offer that's so much better than the love I pour out on you day after day?' And already she panicked at the very thought of having to explain Roger. She would not say 'him', she would say 'us', for she was quite unable to dissociate their two lives. She did not know why. Possibly because the efforts – the painful, unceasing efforts – which she had made for their love these six years had finally come to mean more to her than happiness. Possibly because her pride would not stand for their proving useless; it had grown so used to taking knocks that slowly but surely it had fed on them until finally it had chosen and anointed Roger as its chief scourge. In the end he had always escaped her. And this unpropitious fight had become the reason for her existence.

Yet she was not made for struggling; at times she told herself as much, rubbing Simon's soft, silken, flowing hair up the wrong way. She could, she murmured to him, have glided through life like her hand through his hair. They would lie like this for long hours in the dark night, until at last they fell asleep. They would hold hands and whisper, so that at times she had the ridiculous feeling that she was fourteen again and lying next to a classmate in one of those ghostly dormitories where girls talked under their breath of God and men. She would whisper and Simon, enchanted by this suggestion of mystery, would lower his voice too.

'How would you have lived?'

'I'd have stayed with Marc, my husband. He was nice at heart. Very much in the social swim. And he had too much money . . . I wanted to try . . .'

She attempted to explain it to him. How her life had abruptly assumed the shape of a life, purely as a result of choice, the day she had plunged into the complex, exacting, humiliating world of the professional woman. The intrigues, the material worries, the smiles, the silences. Simon listened, trying to disentangle from these reminiscences something which had a bearing on his love.

'And . . . ?'

'And I think that's how I'd have lived. I might have taken to deceiving Marc in a mild sort of way, I don't know. But I'd have had a child. And for that alone . . .'

She broke off. Simon was hugging her. He wanted a child by her: he wanted everything. She laughed, kissed his eyes, and continued: 'But at twenty, things weren't like that. I remember clearly: I had made up my mind to be happy.'

Yes, she remembered clearly. She walked through the streets and over the beaches with the impetuosity of her desire; she never stopped walking, searching for a face, an idea – a prey. The determination to be happy weighed on her, as it had weighed on three generations: there were no obstacles, there would never be enough. Nowadays she aimed, not at acquiring, but merely at keeping. Keeping a job and a man; both had been unchanged for years, yet at thirty-nine she was certain of neither. Simon was dozing beside her. She murmured: 'Darling, are you asleep . . . ?' and these four words partly wakened him, he said no, he pressed against her in the dark, in her scent, in their mingled warmth, wonderfully happy.

17

IT was his thirtieth cigarette. He sensed as much as he stubbed it out in the cluttered ash-tray. He gave a shudder of distaste and switched on the bedside lamp yet again. It was three in the morning and he could not get to sleep. He flung the window open; and the icy air struck at his face and neck so fiercely that he shut it again and leaned against it, as though to 'look at' the cold. Finally he renounced the deserted street, shot a glance in his mirror, and at once looked away again. He did not like what he saw. He took the packet of Gauloises from the bed-side table, thrust one mechanically to his lips, and immediately took it out again. He no longer cared for these mechanical gestures which had always, till now, given life a good deal of its flavour; he no longer cared for these bachelor habits; he no longer cared for the taste of tobacco. He must take himself in hand; he must be ill. Of course, he missed Paule – but that wasn't enough. At this moment she must be asleep in the arms of that spoilt young brat, she had forgotten everything. He, Roger, had only to go out, pick up a woman and drink. As she supposed. For he sensed that she had never valued him at his true worth. She had always thought him boorish and brutal, although he had offered her the best, the solidest part of himself. Woman were like that: they appeared to demand everything and offer everything, they let you bask in complete confidence, and then one fine day they vanished, for the most futile reason. For nothing could be more futile for Paule than an affair with Simon. But at this moment the boy was holding her in his arms, he was bending over her upturned face, over her body, so sweet, so abandoned, so . . . He spun round, lit his cigarette at last, inhaling the smoke with furious avidity, then emptied the ash-tray into the fireplace. He should have made a fire; Paule used to light one every time she came; she would kneel in front of it, watching the flames spread, helping them along from time to time with one of her wonderfully calm, adroit movements, then she rose, withdrew a little, and the room became pink and shadowy and full of movement, he wanted to make love and he told her so. But that was some time ago. How long was it since Paule had stopped coming? Two years, three perhaps. He had fallen into the habit of calling at her place: it was easier; she was waiting for him.

He was still holding the ash-tray. He let it fall. It rolled over the floor, intact. He would have liked it to smash, to emerge from its inertia; he would have liked breakage and debris. But it did not smash; ash-trays broke only in novels and films; for that, he would have needed one of those small, costly glass ash-trays which cluttered Paule's flat and not this solid Prisunic variety. He must have smashed at least a hundred assorted objects at Paule's – she always laughed. The last time, it had been an enchanting crystal glass which had given whisky an unusual bronze colour. Everything, for that matter, was pleasing to look at in that flat, where he had been lord and master. Everything was coherent, subdued, and calm. Yet he had imagined he was regaining his freedom each time he came out into the night. And now he was alone in his flat, filled with useless rage for an unbreakable ash-tray. He went back to bed, switched off the light, and momentarily admitted his unhappiness before falling asleep with his hand over his heart.

18

THEY met in the doorway of a restaurant one evening, and all three of them executed a classical and absurd little ballet, of a type so frequent in Paris: she gave a distant nod to the man on whose shoulder she had groaned, sighed, and slept; he returned it gracelessly and Simon stared at him without obeying an impulse to hit him. They sat at tables some way apart and she chose from the menu without looking up. For the proprietor and the handful of customers who knew Paule, the scene was entirely commonplace. Simon ordered drinks in a decisive voice, and Roger, at another table, asked his companion which cocktail she preferred. Finally Paule did look up, smiled at Simon, and threw a glance at Roger. She loved him. The fact had struck her the moment she had seen him in the doorway, with the usual set look on his face: she still loved him, she was emerging from a long, useless sleep. He in turn looked at her, then he essayed a smile which instantly froze.

'What will you have?' said Simon. 'White?'

'Why not?'

She stared at her hands on the table, the neatly arranged cutlery, Simon's sleeve beside her bare arm. She drank very fast. Simon was talking without his usual animation. He seemed to expect something from her – or from Roger. Could she get up and say to him: 'Excuse me,' could she walk across the room and say to Roger: 'That's enough, let's go home'? It wasn't done. Come to that, nothing intelligent or sensitive was done nowadays.

After dinner, they danced. She saw Roger with a brunette in his arms – not too bad, for once – Roger swaying in front of her with his usual awkwardness. Simon stood up; he danced well, almost with his eyes shut; he was slim and lithe; she let herself go. At one point her bare arm brushed against Roger's hand, flattened against the brunette's back; she opened her eyes. They looked at each other, Roger, Paule, each behind the 'other's' back. It was a static, rhythmless slow foxtrot. They gazed at one another from a range of four inches, without expression, without smiling, without recognition, it seemed; then suddenly Roger's hand left the brunette's back, reached towards Paule's arm and lightly stroked it with his fingertips, and there was such an imploring expression on his face that she shut her eyes. Simon turned and they lost sight of each other.

That night she refused to sleep with Simon, pleading a tiredness she did not feel. She lay in her bed, for a long time, open-eyed. She knew what was going to happen; she knew that there was not, there never had been, any other possible solution, and she resigned herself to it, in the dark, with a faint tightening of the throat. In the middle of the night she got up and went into the drawing-room, where Simon lay asleep on the divan. By the slanting light from her room she saw the young man's outstretched body and the rise and fall of his breath. She stared at his head buried in the pillow and the small furrow between the bones at the back of his neck; she stared at her own youth sleeping. But when he turned groaning towards the light, she fled. Already she dared not speak to him again.

Next morning, Roger's *pneumatique* was waiting for her at the office. 'I must see you, this can't go on. Ring me.' She rang him. They arranged to meet at six. But ten minutes later, he was there. Huge, in this woman's shop, completely in a maze. She came towards him and showed him into a tiny salon congested with gilt cane-seat chairs: a nightmare setting. Only then did she see him. It was really he. He took a step towards her and put his two hands on her shoulders. He stammered a little, for him a sign of extreme emotion.

'I was so unhappy,' he said.

'Me too,' she heard herself saying, and resting lightly against him she finally began to cry, inwardly begging Simon to forgive her for those two words.

He had laid his head on her hair, he was saying: 'There, there, don't cry,' in a stupid voice.

'I tried,' she said at last, with a note of apology, 'I really did try . . .'

Then she reflected that it was not to him that she ought to be saying this, but to Simon. She was getting muddled. One had always to be on one's guard, could never say everything to the same person. She went on crying, stony-faced. He was silent.

'Say something,' she murmured.

'I was so lonely,' he said. 'I've been thinking things over. Sit down here and take my handkerchief. I'll explain.'

He explained. He explained that one had to keep an eye on women, that he had been rash, and that he realized the whole thing was his fault. He did not hold her irresponsibility against her. They would say no more about it. She said: 'Yes, yes, yes, Roger,' and she felt like crying still more and roaring with laughter. At the same time, she inhaled the familiar smell of his body, of his tobacco, and she felt saved. And lost.

*

Ten days later, she was alone in the flat with Simon for the last time.

'You're forgetting these,' she said.

She held out two ties; she did not look at him; she felt worn out. She had been helping him pack his luggage for nearly two hours now. The light luggage of a young man hopelessly in love but hopelessly untidy. And everywhere they found Simon's lighter, Simon's books, Simon's shoes. He had said nothing, he had conducted himself well and he was aware of it – and that was choking him.

'That's enough,' he said. 'You can leave the rest with your concierge.'

She did not answer. He looked about him, trying to think: 'The last time, the last time,' but he could not manage it. He was shaking nervously.

'I shan't forget,' said Paule, and she raised her eyes to meet his.

'Neither shall I. But that's a different thing,' he said, 'a different thing altogether . . .'

And he wavered, midway to the door, before turning his distraught face on her. Once again she was sustaining him in her arms, she was sustaining his grief as she had sustained his happiness. And she could not help envying him the violence of his grief: a noble grief, a noble pain, such as she would never feel again. He broke away abruptly and rushed out, abandoning his luggage. She followed him, leaned over the banister and called his name: 'Simon! Simon!' and she added without knowing why: 'Simon, I'm old now, old . . .'

But he did not hear her. He was running down the stairs with his eyes full of tears; he was running as though he were cock-a-hoop; he was twenty-five. She shut the door quietly and leaned her back against it.

At eight o'clock, the telephone rang. Even before she answered it, she knew what she was going to hear.

'Forgive me,' said Roger. 'I have a business dinner. I'll be round later. Has . . . ?'